They want the hidden fortune, and they'll kill Tara to get it. This time, even Flynn and her ghosts may not be able to save her.

TARA SAW THE old black pickup as it passed her, but thought nothing of it. When her cell phone rang, and she saw it was Flynn, the pickup was quickly forgotten.

"Hey, Flynn."

"Hey, honey, I meant to call before kickoff, and now it's about to happen. I knew you'd be glued to the set so I thought I'd better talk fast."

She laughed. "I'm not even home. I got sick of being in the house and went for a walk."

Millicent's voice was suddenly screaming in her ear. *Run, Tara run!*

She heard tires screeching on the street behind her and spun around, thinking someone was about to have a wreck. Instead, she saw a man jump out of the same black truck that had just passed her a few moments earlier, and he was running toward her. Her heart dropped. It was happening!

"Help! Flynn! It's happening," she screamed, and turned to run, felt a sharp pain in the back of her thigh and dropped into the snow, unable to move or talk, shaking convulsively from the Taser's electrodes.

Flynn heard the tires, her cry for help and the warning, then nothing. She was being abducted! Why wasn't she running? Why was she suddenly silent? Why wasn't he picking up on her thoughts anymore? God in heaven, what had they done to her?

His heart was hammering so hard against his chest that he thought he'd pass out, but he knew exactly what was happening. Her nightmare was coming true, and he was too far away to help.

The Novels of Sharon Sala from Bell Bridge Books

The Lunatic Life Series

My Lunatic Life

Lunatic Detective

Lunatic Revenge

Lunatic Times Two

The Boarding House

Lunatic Times Two

Book 4 of the LUNATIC LIFE Series

by

Sharon Sala

Bell Bridge Books

This is a work of fiction. Names, characters, places and incidents are either the products of the author's imagination or are used fictitiously. Any resemblance to actual persons (living or dead), events or locations is entirely coincidental.

Bell Bridge Books
PO BOX 300921
Memphis, TN 38130
Print ISBN: 978-1-61194-362-7

Bell Bridge Books is an Imprint of BelleBooks, Inc.

Printed and bound in the United States of America.

We at BelleBooks enjoy hearing from readers.
Visit our websites – www.BelleBooks.com and www.BellBridgeBooks.com.

10 9 8 7 6 5 4 3 2 1

Cover design: Debra Dixon
Interior design: Hank Smith
Photo/Art credits:
Girl (manipulated) © Chaoss | Dreamstime.com
Background (manipulated) © Andrey Kiselev | Dreamstime.com

:Ltlt:01:

Dedication

The best part about really knowing someone is the uniqueness that is theirs alone. No one is born alike; not even identical twins. Having a friend is even better because they don't care what you look like, or what you can or can't do. They like you simply because you are you.

The little heroine in this Lunatic Life series hasn't always had the luxury of friends or the acceptance of just being herself until she and her uncle move to Oklahoma. It was there she found people who didn't mind that she could see and talk to spirits. It was the first time in her life that she felt like she belonged.

I want to dedicate not only this book, but all four of the Lunatic Life books to the people who go through life marching to the beat of a drum only they can hear. Being different is what makes you special. It is a very good thing.

Chapter One

TARA COULDN'T breathe, and despite how fiercely she was fighting, the hands around her throat kept squeezing tighter and tighter. Her field of vision had narrowed to the emotionless expression on the pockmarked face of the man above her. No matter how many times her punches landed, or how hard she bucked and kicked trying to throw him off her body, it had no effect. His sole purpose was to end her life at any expense, and it appeared he was willing to suffer to make that happen. Even after there was no breath left in her to make a sound, inside, she was screaming for Flynn.

Help me! Help me!

And then it was too late.

The man's face was fading before her eyes. She could actually feel her spirit leaving her body. When she realized she was floating above, a wave of sadness swept through her. She saw her lifeless body below.

I wasn't ready to die.

Tara! Tara! Wake up! It's just a dream!

Flynn, is that you?

"TARA! TARA! Wake up! You're having a bad dream!"

Tara woke up with a gasp then took a deep breath, shocked she could actually breathe. She wasn't dead after all. Thank God, thank God!

Her uncle, Pat Carmichael, put a hand on her forehead to test for a fever.

"Are you sick, honey?"

"No, I'm fine, Uncle Pat. It was just a crazy dream."

"Good. I have to go in to work early. They are going to

need all hands on deck at the city barn today to help sand the streets."

"Why? You don't work on Saturday."

"It's snowing, and from the look of the roads, it's been snowing most of the night. I'm glad there's no school. You stay inside and stay warm. Gotta go. Call if you need me," he said, and blew her a kiss as he hurried away.

She threw back the covers and ran to the windows. A heavy snow was falling, and even though the reality of her dream was beginning to fade, the horror of it was still with her. She leaned her forehead against the cold windowpane and shuddered. As she turned away, she glanced toward her dresser to the picture of her boyfriend, Flynn. The fact that he had been able to mentally enter her nightmare and pull her out of it was shocking. She was still struggling with how he'd changed after his accident. He'd come out of the coma—from the brink of death—with the ability to hear thoughts—even hers.

Moon girl?

Tara spun around, but there was no one there.

Flynn?

Are you awake now?

Yes. OMG! This is going to take some getting used to, having you hear my thoughts. Did I scare you?

No. I could tell you were dreaming.

Really? How?

I don't know. I just could. Stay inside and stay warm. Love you.

Tara put a hand over her heart as a big smile broke over her face.

I love you, too.

A pink puff of smoke drifted across Tara's line of vision.

What about me? I loved you first.

Tara's smile widened as the ghost who'd helped raise her injected herself into the conversation.

"Of course I love you, Millicent. I love you and Henry to death."

You need not put that much effort into the relationship, Tara. We're already dead.

Tara rolled her eyes. "You know what I mean."

Henry, the other ghost who was part of her life, popped up in the middle of Tara's bed wearing a coonskin cap and dressed in buckskins.

"Henry?"

He saluted, blew her a kiss, and floated toward the ceiling in a horizontal position, with the tail of the cap hanging down behind his neck like a rudder on an outboard motor.

Tara watched him floating, trying to figure out what was going on now. With Henry, it was always a bit hard to tell.

"What on earth is Henry doing?"

I think he's reliving one of his past lives. He was a fur trapper once. I haven't been able to get him out of that ridiculous cap. If he wants to wear fur, he should go for something elegant, like mink, or ermine. I had an ermine coat once. A Russian prince gave it to me then insisted I wear it, and nothing else, to bed.

Tara shrieked and put her hands over her ears. "OMG, Millicent! What part of 'too much information' do you not understand?" She grabbed a change of clothes and headed to the bathroom. After this rude awakening, there was no way she was going back to bed.

Later, she settled down in front of the television with a cup of hot chocolate and a piece of buttered toast as breakfast, absently watching the programming as she dunked and ate. A few cars went by on the street outside the house, but none were going fast. Some were even having trouble navigating. She watched them sliding sideways. She thought of Uncle Pat having to work in this weather and began thinking of what she could make for supper that would be hot and filling; she wondered where their crock pot was. She remembered unpacking it when they moved here, but hadn't used it since.

Tara dug through the cabinets until she found the crock pot, then started a stew for supper. After that, it was down to the weekly chore of cleaning the house and sorting laundry.

A couple of hours later, she was making a grocery list and listening to the radio when the phone began to ring.

It was Nikki, her BFF.

"Hi, Nikki. What's going on?"

"Rachelle and Morgan are outside trying to make a snowman, but the snow isn't sticking, and they're basically just freezing themselves for the heck of it."

Tara laughed. "Isn't that what kids are supposed to do? And why aren't you out there with them?"

Nikki sighed. "I have a sore throat. Mom won't let me."

Tara frowned. "Bummer, Nik. Do you have a fever, too?"

"No, at least not right now. I sure hope I'm not getting sick with the flu. It's going around town like crazy. Mom said there are three out of her office with it, and Dad's got two out in his office."

"Ick," Tara muttered. "At least stay warm and dry, and I'll see you at school."

"Call me later. I'll be bored."

Tara was still smiling as she hung up and went to get the clothes out of the dryer before they wrinkled.

A short time later, she was hanging up the last of Uncle Pat's work shirts in his closet when she felt a presence. The hair rose on the backs of her arms, and there was a pressure on her chest, like she was being pushing backward. She turned abruptly, quickly stifling a gasp.

There was a woman standing in the doorway wringing her hands, and Tara could see through her to the picture hanging on the wall in the hall behind her. Except for Millicent and Henry, there hadn't been a ghost in this house since DeeDee Broyles, who had been in residence when they moved in, and she'd long since gone into the light.

This woman's voice was shrill and shaking.

You can see me, can't you?

Tara nodded.

Oh, thank God. They said you could, but I wasn't sure.

Tara frowned. "They? Who's they?"

A pink puff of smoke swirled into view.

That would be Henry and me. Sorry, but she has a problem you need to fix.

Tara groaned. "Millicent! Are you serious? There's a

blizzard outside. I have no car. What can I possibly do?"

Ask her yourself. Her name is Connie.

Tara frowned. The ghost was a curvy little blonde in a long pink flannel nightgown, and her feet were bare. Not that she could feel the cold anymore, but it told Tara that the woman had probably died in bed.

"So Connie, other than the fact that you're dead, what's wrong?"

Connie wailed. *My husband! My children! They won't wake up. They're dying, too, and I can't find anyone to help.*

All of a sudden a wave of despair slid through Tara so fast there were tears on her face before she knew it.

That's how mother love feels.

Tara thought of her own mother, wondering if she had been in this kind of despair when she died in the wreck that left Tara an orphan.

Yes, that's exactly how your mother felt, but this is no time to dwell on history. Do something! Now!

Millicent's warning made Tara focus.

"Why are they dying, too? What's wrong with them?"

Carbon monoxide! The alarm upstairs is going off, but no one is moving.

Now she understood the need for haste.

"Connie, what's your last name?"

The little blonde wailed. *I don't understand why this is happening, but I can't remember.*

Tara tried another question. "Where do you live?"

Connie was wringing her hands. *I don't remember that either.*

Tara knew death was often confusing. Lots of times spirits didn't even know they were dead, and in the confusion lost memories that had to do with the world of the living.

"We'll come at this from another angle," Tara said. "What do you remember?"

My name is Connie.

Tara groaned.

Millicent interrupted. *She doesn't remember the rest, Tara. The only thing I know that might help is that she works at city hall, because that's where I found her. She was trying to make someone hear her and causing quite a stir. Papers were flying, and the coffee pot exploded. She doesn't know how to control the energy her panic is causing.*

Tara ran for her cell phone and called the police. The fact that she had their number on speed dial was not unusual—for a teenage girl who kept getting herself mixed up in dangerous situations and had psychic talents she couldn't explain.

"Stillwater Police."

"I need to talk to Detective Rutherford or Detective Allen ASAP. Tell them it's Tara Luna calling."

"One moment, please."

Tara glanced at the ghost and the spiral of pink vapor around her head and knew Millicent was trying to calm the little spirit. She was moving into panic mode herself when she heard Detective Rutherford's voice.

"Hey, Tara, this is Detective Rutherford. What's going on?"

"I need you to find out the home address of a woman named Connie who works at city hall, and then dispatch rescue to the house. Her family is dying."

She heard a gasp, then a groan, and sighed. Rutherford was obviously not happy with her.

"How the hel . . . excuse my French . . . do you know this?"

She glanced at the ghost again.

"Well, Connie's spirit is standing in my living room begging me to help her family before they all die, too."

"You're talking to a ghost as we speak?"

Tara rolled her eyes. "No. I'm talking to you, but I'm looking at *her*. She said it's carbon monoxide poisoning, and they won't wake up."

"Why doesn't she tell you her last name and address?" Rutherford muttered.

"Because she doesn't remember that anymore. Please! She has kids and a husband you might be able to save. Hurry!"

"Well, hell . . . excuse me again . . . hang on. I'll make a call and see what happens."

She could hear him yelling at his partner, Detective Allen, and then someone else saying they knew a woman named

Connie in the court clerk's office.

"Connie! Did you work in the court clerk's office?"

I don't know. I have to go! My babies will be looking for me!

All of a sudden she was gone.

"Now what? How can she find her kids when she doesn't know her address?" Tara muttered.

The maternal cord of a mother is forever tied to her children, regardless of where a spirit might be.

Tara felt an instant pang of loss.

"Then why have I never seen my mother and father?" she whispered.

What makes you think you haven't?

Before Tara could pursue that comment, Detective Rutherford was back on the line.

"Okay, we have a name and address and have dispatched a patrol car and ambulances. For once, I hope you're wrong about this."

"Keep me posted, okay?"

Rutherford sighed. "I will. Stay inside. It's cold."

He disconnected.

Tara caught a glimpse of Henry through the window. He was marching back and forth out on the porch with a long rifle cradled in his arms.

"Now what?"

Millicent's voice was in her ear. *He's standing guard.*

Tara stifled a spurt of panic. "Why? Am I in danger again?"

He's on the lookout for other spirits. He thinks you don't need to be bothered anymore. Just ignore him.

Tara shook her head and turned away. No one would believe her life, even if she tried to explain.

She glanced at the clock. It was already past noon, and whatever appetite she might have had was gone. This day was going to be very sad if that whole family died.

She headed for the kitchen to check on the stew. Her day might be in turmoil, but Uncle Pat was still going to be hungry when he came home tonight.

RUTHERFORD HUNG up the phone and grabbed his coat.

"Hey, where are you going?" Allen asked.

Rutherford sighed. "That dang girl has my curiosity up again. I need to see for myself if that family is really in danger. If there's a woman named Connie lying dead in that house, I am never going to doubt Tara Luna again."

Allen snorted softly. "I have heard you say that before, and yet here you are, still doubting and going for another look."

Rutherford was putting on his coat as he walked. "So sue me. Are you coming with me, or not?"

"You know I am, but we're taking your SUV. You've got four-wheel drive," Allen said.

"Then hurry up. The ambulance and patrol cars are probably already there."

They left the police station, buttoning their coats as they went. The moment they stepped outside, the swirling snow and cold hit them like a slap in the face.

"I hate winter," Allen said.

Rutherford grunted as he unlocked the doors and started the engine. A few moments later they were on the street, sliding sideways through intersections, with the windshield wipers swiping uselessly at the swirl of icy snow.

As Rutherford had predicted, the ambulance and a couple of cruisers were already there. When they started toward the house, another detective met them at the door.

"Hey, what are you two doing here? Darrell and I caught this case."

"We took the call," Rutherford said. "Wanted to see for ourselves if it was on the up and up."

The detective shrugged. "It wasn't a hoax, if that's what you're asking, and it's a damn shame. Fire department said carbon monoxide poisoning."

Rutherford felt the skin tightening at the back of his neck just like it always did when he was presented with a truth about Tara Luna's abilities he couldn't ignore.

Allen was brushing snow off his coat. "Any survivors?" he asked.

"The woman is dead. Her husband and two kids still have a faint pulse. EMTs are working on them now for transport. Do you want to check out the scene or anything?"

Rutherford shook his head. "No. I only look at dead people when somebody makes me."

"Coming through," an EMT shouted.

They stepped back to make room for the gurney and the little girl on it. They had her on oxygen and covered in blankets against the cold. There was a second gurney coming up behind with a slightly older boy. Both children were ghostly pale, but alive.

"Damn shame," Allen said softly. "I sure hope the father survives. It would suck if those kids lost both their parents."

"Let's get out of here," Rutherford said. "We can check on their welfare back at the station."

They ran to the car and jumped inside, shivering from the wind's icy blast. Rutherford started up the SUV and drove away.

"Hey, the police station is that way," Allen said, pointing to the left as Rutherford took a right.

"Thought I'd go by Tara's house to let her know she was right."

Allen snorted softly. "She already knows she's right. You're the one who keeps on doubting her. I'm staying in the car."

Rutherford's eyes narrowed as a gust of wind sent the snow swirling around the vehicle, making it appear as if they were driving in an arctic tornado. Just for a moment he wondered if it was one of Tara's ghosts doing that, then decided that was stupid and kept driving.

He didn't know that Millicent was in the back seat, admiring the cut of Rutherford's jaw. She was fond of manly men, and these two fit her notion of manly just fine.

WHEN TARA WAS troubled, she baked. And after the visit from the sad ghost, Tara was more than troubled. If those kids lived, they were going to wake up and find out their mother was dead.

She'd gone to the kitchen with a heavy heart and began stirring up cookie dough to stay occupied. She was already taking oatmeal raisin cookies out of the oven when someone began knocking. She set the tray aside and grabbed a towel, wiping her hands as she went, then peeked through the window before opening the door.

"Detective Rutherford, come in."

He stepped inside, shivering noticeably as he shut the door behind him.

"Thank you. It's miserable out there."

"I didn't expect to see you. Are you by yourself?" she asked.

"No, Allen's in the car. I wanted to apologize for giving you a hard time about your phone call. Maybe one of these days I'll learn to act without asking you questions."

"It's okay."

"No, it's not. I don't know how this will ultimately turn out, but the dad and two kids were still alive when we found them, and you can take credit for that."

Tara heard a pop and saw the little barefoot spirit holding her hands against her breasts and smiling.

Tell him thank you.

"I will," Tara said.

Rutherford frowned. "You will what?"

"Oh, sorry. I was talking to Connie."

Rutherford eyed the room with a nervous glance. "So, you're saying her spirit is here?"

"Yes. There," she said, pointing to a spot beside Rutherford.

He jumped like he'd been goosed and landed right where Tara was pointing. When the hair suddenly stood up on the backs of his arms, he moaned. "I'm standing on her, aren't I?" he whispered.

"Well, let's just say you're both sharing the same space."

"Excuse me, Connie," he whispered, and took four quick steps backward.

"You didn't hurt her," Tara said, as she watched the little ghost beginning to lose substance. "She wants me to tell you how grateful she is that you helped save her family."

All of a sudden there were tears in Rutherford's eyes. "I'm sorry we couldn't save her," he said softly.

Tara could hear Connie's voice, but it was getting fainter. She was already moving toward the light.

"She's not sorry. She says that she had to die to come find help, or they would have all perished."

He took out a handkerchief and blew his nose. "Dang cold wind made my nose run," he said.

Tara felt like crying with him and changed the subject. "I made cookies. Would you like some?"

The fact that she'd not only changed the subject but offered food was good.

"Yeah, that would be great!" he said.

"I'll send enough for you to share with Detective Allen."

"Don't send him more than a couple. He was too big of a coward to come in."

Tara laughed, then stopped and tilted her head.

"What's wrong?" Rutherford asked.

"Your partner is going to wish he'd come inside with you."

"Why?"

Millicent is in the backseat of your car messing with him. He's not sure what's happening, but he's getting rattled."

Rutherford's eyes widened. "Make sure she stays *here* when we leave, okay?"

Tara smiled. "I'll mention it to her, but she pretty much does what she wants."

"Oh lord, lord," Rutherford muttered.

"I'll get the cookies," Tara said, and hurried to the kitchen and bagged up a half-dozen.

When she got back to the living room, Allen was standing by his partner. His eyes were wide, and the expression on his face was somewhat shell-shocked.

"Someone was pulling on my hair," he whispered, and glanced around the room as if he were about to be attacked.

"I'm sorry," Tara said. "If she does it again, just tell her to stop and leave you alone. She has to obey. It's part of the rules on the other side."

"*Now* you tell us," Rutherford muttered. "Thanks a lot for the cookies. We better get going."

"You're welcome," Tara said, as she walked them to the door.

She heard a loud pop. Millicent was ticked.

You didn't have to tell them about the rules.

Tara closed the door behind the two men. "And you didn't have to bother him. You knew he was going to freak. You did it on purpose."

Whatever.

There was another loud pop, a large puff of pink smoke, and Millicent was gone.

"Whatever, yourself," Tara said, and headed back to the kitchen to finish the cookies.

Chapter Two

THE COOKIES WERE cooling on the rack, and Tara was asleep on the sofa with an old patch-work quilt pulled up beneath her chin. Outside, the snow was still coming down, and the wind was causing it to drift. The electricity flickered off then came back on again.

Millicent was perched on the back of the sofa keeping watch over Tara as she slept, while Henry was hovering between the living room and the kitchen, wishing he could still smell and eat. The stew bubbling in the crock pot looked enticing.

An old pickup truck with a load of firewood piled high in the truck bed drove past the house. It was the fourth time it had circled the block, which was why Millicent was keeping watch. She and Henry knew the person behind the wheel was up to no good, but they weren't sure if Tara was a specific target. Until then, they would not interfere.

It was close to four p.m. when the phone rang. Tara threw back the covers and reached for the receiver even before her eyes were fully open.

"Hello?"

"Hey, honey, it's me. I'm heading home. Checking to see if I need to bring supper."

"Hi, Uncle Pat. No, don't bring food. I made stew. It should be done by five."

"Stew sounds so good. Do you need anything?"

"Not a thing. You just come home and get warm."

"On my way."

When he disconnected, Tara got up, folded up her covers and then headed for the kitchen, pausing in the hall to turn up the thermostat. The house was chilly, which meant it must be getting colder outside. The good news was, it had stopped snowing.

She had cornbread baking in the oven, and coffee was brewing, when she heard the front door open.

"I'm home!" Pat called.

"In the kitchen!" she yelled back.

Pat popped in long enough to give her a kiss and peek at the stew. "This looks so good," he said. "I won't be long, but I need to change into some dry clothes."

"I did laundry, so your sweats are clean."

He gave her a thumbs up. "I'll be right back."

Tara began to set the table, adding butter and molasses for the cornbread. Uncle Pat liked cornbread with stew, and cornbread with molasses for dessert, so she knew he was going to make a sizeable dent in the pan still baking.

A few minutes later he was back. "What can I do to help?"

"Just pour yourself a cup of coffee and sit and talk to me."

He took his coffee to the table, stirred in some cream and sugar, and then leaned back, watching her work. She reminded him so much of his sister, Shirley, right down to the long legs and dark hair. All of their family was tall; the fact that Tara was like her mother was no exception.

"So what did you do today?" he asked.

Although what happened this morning wasn't a secret, she wanted him to hear it from her.

"I have to say it was quite a morning. I was doing laundry and cleaning when the spirit of a woman who'd just died popped up, begging me to help save her family."

Pat's hands tightened around the coffee cup, but other than that, he didn't react to what she was saying. However, he could tell by the expression on her face that she'd been shaken, which was unusual.

"How tragic, honey. Was it a traffic accident?"

"No, it was carbon monoxide in their home. She was frantic, trying to find someone to help before her husband and children died, too."

"Dear God," Pat said softly, and leaned forward, resting his elbows on the table as she continued the story.

"To make a sad story short, we found out her name and address, and the police rescued the family. I haven't heard anything more, but they were still alive when they found them."

"Then that's good, right? She accomplished her task and moved on. She did move on, right?"

Tara nodded then took the cornbread out of the oven and cut it into squares, then began dishing up the stew. She piled a platter full of the crusty yellow squares and carried it to the table.

"Yes, she's gone, but when it was all happening, I could feel how frantic she was, and how much she loved them."

Pat frowned. "Well, sure, honey. Any parent would be frantic."

She carried the bowls of stew to the table, setting one at her place and one at his then went back for the cornbread. Even as she sat, Pat could tell there was more.

"Do you think my mother and father felt like that?" she asked.

Pat stifled a groan. So that was it. He reached for her hand and gave it a squeeze. "Oh, honey, you don't even have to ask. There was never a mother more proud of her child than Shirley was of you."

Tara's eyes were glistening with unshed tears. "I can see spirits all the time. They're around me no matter where we go, and yet I've never seen my mom or dad. They've never even tried to talk to me."

"How do you know?"

She frowned. That was almost the same thing Millicent had said earlier. "I don't know, but I would have thought they would at least have identified themselves."

Pat sighed. He didn't like to admit he'd grown up in a house full of psychics, but he knew enough to answer some of her questions. "I don't know how the other side works, but I can remember my mom and Shirley talking about it some. Their rules are different than ours, right?"

She nodded.

"So maybe they aren't allowed to pop up and say, 'Hi, I'm Mom. How's it going?' You were so little when they died that maybe you just never had time to form a bond that would help you recognize them from this side. Do you know what I mean?"

Tara's eyes widened. "Yes, I do, and that makes sense. I never thought of it that way."

He smiled. "Then for now let's agree that you were loved, and still are loved to distraction. You saved some lives today, this stew smells wonderful, and I'm starved. How's that?"

She smiled. "Good." She took a bite of the stew. "Needs salt," she added, and passed the shaker.

After that, the conversation was less serious. She listened absently as he talked about the snowdrifts and the streets they'd sanded and the cars stranded all over town. It wasn't until she'd carried away their empty bowls and was running water in them at the sink, that her uncle shifted the conversation again.

"It's just a couple of days until New Year's, and then you'll be back in school."

Tara nodded. "I know. I can't believe that I'll finally be graduating high school. Growing up is exciting and just a little bit scary."

"No scarier than it is for me. Some days I don't want to face the fact that you will get married and move away from me."

She frowned. "Well, I can promise you that will be down the road a few years, so stop dwelling on that, okay?"

"Okay." He was silent a few moments as he continued to eat. When he finished his stew, he pushed the bowl aside and then leaned forward. "So . . . if I took Mona to a New Year's Eve party, how would you feel about that?"

Tara frowned. "What do you mean, 'How would I feel?' I'd feel fine. That's a weird question."

He shrugged and reached for another square of cornbread, then began drenching it in molasses. "We seem to be putting down some roots here in Stillwater, and I thought it might be a good idea if I got to know some people. She wanted to go and asked me. I told her it depended on what the dress code was. She laughed, but I was serious. I don't own nice clothes."

"Oh, Uncle Pat! I can help you with that. After we get groceries at Walmart tomorrow, we can swing by some of the clothing stores. It's not a formal party, is it?"

"No, but she said anything I might wear to church would be fine, but as you know, that's yet another thing I've failed you on. We don't go to church. The older you get, the more I am beginning to realize that your life has been negatively impacted by me and my failures to provide."

Tara strode over to the table and threw her arms around his neck, hugging him fiercely. "That is so not true, and I don't ever want to hear you talk bad about yourself to me again."

He patted her arm. "It's apparent there are holes in your social life because we moved so much."

Tara laughed. "Uncle Pat, get serious. There are holes in my social life because of who and what I am. Not because we moved around. Now, tomorrow we go shopping, and that's that."

She hugged him again and then got a small plate and a piece of cornbread and sat down.

Pat arched an eyebrow, popped a bite of his cornbread and molasses into his mouth and then shoved the thick, sweet syrup across the table. "I might want another piece of cornbread," he said as she tilted the jar, eying the amount of dark syrup pouring freely onto her plate.

"Chill, Uncle Pat. It's over half-full."

His bushy eyebrows knitted over the bridge of his nose as he watched it continue to flow. "Ummhmm, I see it."

She laughed, and just to make him nervous, poured an extra dollop on the plate, then shoved it back toward him.

He laughed. "You are something else, girl."

A couple of spoons banged in the sink.

He jumped. "What was that?"

Tara glanced over her shoulder. "It's just Henry checking out the stew. He wants to taste it, but unfortunately for Henry, ghosts don't eat."

"Lord," Pat muttered swiped a bite of cornbread through

the molasses, and popped it in his mouth.

Tara laughed. Right now, her lunatic life felt just about perfect.

SNOW HAD DRIFTED behind the old black pickup and onto the load of wood in the bed, concealing everything but the front part of the cab and the hood. The windshield wipers were frozen to the window, and the battery was dead because the driver, Vince Dudley, had tried to start the truck so many times after it stalled that he'd run it down. Now he sat huddled behind the wheel with his coat collar pulled up around his ears, cursing the weather and his boss for sending him out in this mess.

When he saw a small pair of headlights suddenly appear out of the dark, Vince breathed a shaky sigh of relief. It would suck eggs to freeze to death on this wild-goose chase here in the States, tracking down some stupid teenager who supposedly saw ghosts. Michael O'Mara was dead, and wherever he'd buried that damn drug money, it would most likely stay buried for eternity. If Vince had his druthers, he'd pack up and go back home to Canada.

He jumped out in the snowdrift, cursing softly as the snow went up past his knees, and began waving his arms as the old John Deere tractor came near.

Boots Digby pulled up to the snowbound truck and turned around until he was facing the other way, then got out of the tractor cab and waded through the snow. "Man, this stuff is deep here."

Vince didn't bother to comment. He wanted to get back to the house. "Did you bring a chain?"

"Yep, yep I did," Dig said, returned to the tractor, and unwound the large coil of chain on the back.

"Here, give it to me," Vince said. "I'm so cold I can't feel my feet." Vince dug through the snow beneath his truck to get to the front axle and hooked the chain around it. He got up, brushing snow off his clothes as he crawled back into the truck.

Dig had already hooked his end of the chain to the tractor

and was patiently waiting for Vince to get back in the truck. When he did, Dig put the tractor in gear and moved forward slowly until the chain was fully extended, then began the laborious process of pulling Vince and his vehicle back to the house.

The house belonged to May Schulter, who'd been part of the gang Michael O'Mara belonged to when he was arrested and sent to prison. Their boss, Marshall Story, was May's only child. She'd given him up at birth, never knowing what became of him: that he was adopted and raised in Canada.

It was only a few years back that they'd reconnected and ever since kept up a relationship through letters and phone calls. When all of the mess with Flynn and the Nettles gang was going down, she'd told him everything, including the fact that the money in question was close to a half million dollars, and she was looking for a psychic to help her find it. Then she got herself arrested, and they lost touch. Afterward, he'd thought and thought about all that money just waiting to be found, until it was driving him crazy. When he mentioned it to Vince and Dig, their excitement fed his interest, until they found themselves leaving Canada and on the way to Oklahoma to find it.

They arrived and found May's house with no problem. The condition it was in had been staggering, but it was too far to go back without at least giving their plan a try. So they did their investigating, finally located the psychic, only to have the weather become an issue. Their visitor visas would expire soon, and, blizzard or not, they had to act fast or back out.

Vince's fingers were so cold it was difficult to grip the steering wheel, so when his cell rang, he almost didn't answer. Then he saw it was Marsh and picked up.

"This is Vince."

"Did Dig find you?"

"Yeah. We're about a mile and a half from the house, and I'm nearly frozen."

"Coffee's hot, and there's some chili on the stove. We'll talk when you get here."

The line went dead.

"Yeah, goodbye to you, too," Vince muttered, and dropped the phone in his pocket.

THE FEATHERS ON the dream-catcher hanging on the wall above Tara's bed shifted slightly as the heating unit kicked on, sending a rush of warm air into the room. Tara moaned softly as she rolled over in her sleep.

Millicent hovered at the foot of her bed while Henry continued to keep watch outside. They knew she was in danger, but didn't know when it would happen or where it would come from. They had decided between them to tell her in the morning. Even if it did frighten her, it was better for her to be forewarned.

While they were keeping watch, Tara was far from having a restful sleep. Once again, she'd fallen back into the same dream she'd had the night before and was running from the man with the pockmarked face, knowing that he would catch her before she could reach her phone, and knowing that she would die.

She was screaming for help when a voice forcefully entered her dream.

Wake up, Tara! Wake up!

Tara was gasping for air when she heard the voice. Her eyes flew open. The pockmarked man was nowhere in sight, and she was safe in her bed. She rolled over onto her back then sat up.

Flynn?

Yes, it's me, Moon Girl. Same dream?

Yes. I'm scared, Flynn. I think I'm going to die.

Don't say that, damn it!

I can't help what I see.

It's a dream. It doesn't have to come true.

Tara combed the hair from her face with shaky fingers.

Tara?

I'm still here.

I'm coming to see you tomorrow.

She thought about the upcoming shopping trip.

Then I'll come, after you and Pat get home.

She blinked. *You heard me thinking about that, too?*

Sorry. I'm so tuned into you it's automatic, and I don't know how to turn this off yet.

Don't apologize. Just come see me.

I'll be there. Go to sleep, Moon Girl. I've got your back.

Tara shuddered.

We're here, too, honey. Go to sleep.

Tara's chin quivered as her eyes filled with tears. "Am I going to die, Millicent?"

We all die.

Tara's heart skipped. "Are you saying that my life is in danger?"

We were saving that for in the morning, but yes, Henry and I feel it. We just don't know who or why.

Instead of increasing her fear, the verification of what she'd been seeing just made Tara mad. "Well, that's just great. Why couldn't I have been born normal, like everyone else? Being me is like living with a target painted on my back. I can't turn around without ticking someone off or running into creeps."

If you hadn't been born as you are, Connie's family would be dead, and so would a whole lot of other people you helped rescue after the tornado earlier this year. Not only that, but Flynn would never have been able to come out of the coma after the accident you two were in. Everything comes at a price. You're not dead yet. Stop whining, pay attention, and I would assume it can be prevented.

Tara's anger shifted. It was rare that Millicent ever scolded her, which made it all the more pertinent.

"You're right. I'm sorry," she whispered.

Go have some milk and cookies—and eat one for Henry and me. We won't be far.

Tara threw back the covers, slipped into her house shoes, and pulled a hoodie over her pajama top as she headed down the hall. She paused in the living room, then moved to the front windows and shoved the curtains aside to peer out into the darkness.

Snow blanketed the houses and streets. The wind had

finally quieted, but not before it blew massive drifts against the north sides of all the houses and cars. Uncle Pat was going to have to shovel their car out before they could get anywhere tomorrow. It looked so peaceful, and yet she knew better than most that evil lurked, always looking for the weak and unprepared. Well, she wasn't weak, and she was no longer unprepared.

She let the curtains fall back in place as she headed to the kitchen and turned on the light. The worn blue and white tiles on the floor were clean and shiny. The dishes were done and put away. Everything was in its place. It felt safe to go farther. She poured herself a glass of milk and got a couple of cookies out of the cookie jar, then settled down at the kitchen table to eat.

She'd just taken her first bite when Henry popped up, still in his buckskins and coonskin cap, looking wistfully at the cookies. She smiled.

"I'm sorry. They're chewy, oatmeal raisin cookies with a hint of cinnamon. Do you remember that?"

He nodded and rubbed his stomach.

She took another bite and leaned back, eyeing his outfit thoughtfully. "Did you ever know Daniel Boone?"

He nodded and clapped his hands together, indicating they had been buddies.

She thought about the stories she'd read and the song people had made up about Daniel.

"Did Daniel Boone really kill a bear when he was only three years old?"

Henry shook his head no.

"I didn't think so," Tara muttered.

He held up four fingers.

She laughed. "Oh, so he was really four years old and not three?"

Henry winked.

"You're not going to tell me, are you?"

He shook his head and disappeared, but by then, Tara was in a much better mood. She finished the cookies and milk, rinsed the glass and put it in the sink, then turned out the light and went back to bed.

Just before she closed her eyes, she thought she saw a puff of pink smoke by the window and sighed. *Millicent.* She might be in danger, but she had her own brand of backup. It was enough to give her peace of mind.

Chapter Three

THE SKY WAS clear the next day, and the sunshine was blinding on all the snow. Someone had cleaned off the Walmart parking lot, then salted and sanded the walkways to make it safe for shoppers to come and go. From the number of cars in the lot, it appeared half the county was inside.

"Oh my gosh, Uncle Pat. We're going to have to park all the way at the back of the lot."

"No, there's one," he said, and took a quick turn down the next aisle and wheeled into the empty spot a car length ahead of another shopper.

"Do you have the grocery list?" he asked.

She patted her pocket.

"Then let's get at it."

The air was so cold that when they got out, she felt like running as they headed across the parking lot. Her steps were long and swift, and her dark hair bounced in rhythm to her steps. She was a tall girl and would have been noticeable anyway in her bright yellow hoodie and skinny-leg black jeans, but after her rescue efforts in the aftermath of the tornado a couple of months ago, nearly everyone knew she was the girl who saw ghosts. It made for interesting shopping experiences, and there was nothing she could do about it.

As soon as they went to get a shopping cart, Uncle Pat realized they were being watched. He frowned and moved closer to her.

"It's okay, Uncle Pat. Don't pay any attention to them. I'll be fine. I can't hide. We live here. Besides, Henry and Millicent have a good handle on refocusing people's attitudes."

He grinned. "Yeah, like scaring them silly."

"Whatever works," she said, and grabbed a cart. "It's not on the list, but if you get some marshmallow fluff and a bag of chocolate chips, I'll make fudge."

He nodded as he pulled a cart out of the stack. "Oh, I'm all over that."

They took a left toward the grocery section with Pat pushing the cart and Tara picking out the produce they needed. She felt the double-takes and stares as they moved through the aisles, but stayed focused on stocking up their pantry.

Her uncle had wandered over to the fruit display to get some apples and bananas, and Tara was choosing a head of lettuce when someone tapped her on the shoulder. She turned to see an older, elegantly dressed woman with diamonds on her fingers and tears in her eyes.

"I'm so sorry to intrude, but are you the girl who sees ghosts?"

Tara felt the woman's agony.

"Yes, ma'am."

"My only child died in the tornado. You helped the rescuers find her body. I just wanted to thank you."

"It was a bad time. I was happy to be of service," Tara said quietly.

The woman nodded, but didn't walk away. Tara knew there was more, and when a spirit suddenly manifested beside the woman, Tara heard the message that needed to be delivered. "She's with you. You know that, don't you?"

The older woman exhaled slowly. "I thought . . . no, I *felt* that was so, but wasn't sure. I've never experienced anything like this before."

Tara glanced at the spirit. She was beautiful, but very sad, which told Tara she hadn't moved on, then quickly got the reason why. "She knows you're sick. She's sorry she won't be here to help take care of you."

"Oh my God, no one knows that," the older woman whispered.

Tara listened, and then nodded. "She also wants you to know that when it's time, she'll be waiting for you."

The woman took a deep, shuddering breath, and then

briefly closed her eyes. As she did, tears ran out from beneath her eyelids and down her face. She dug a tissue from her purse and quickly dried her eyes. "I apologize. I never meant to—"

Tara laid a hand on the woman's arm. "No need. She says to tell you to stop worrying, and that you won't hurt."

The woman gasped. "Dear Lord, child. You are a gift from God. Thank you. Thank you."

She turned away and disappeared into the crowd.

Tara dropped the head of lettuce into the cart and tried not to think of the sadness that had enveloped her. After a few moments, it began to fade.

"Are you through here?" Uncle Pat asked, as he put a couple of bags of fruit into the cart.

She nodded. "On to the cereal aisle."

They moved through the rest of the list without incident and headed to checkout. As usual, the lines were long, and the checkers were working madly trying to keep up.

"We can do self-checkout, Uncle Pat."

"Do you know how to do that?"

"Yes. Were you going to pay with cash or debit card?"

"Debit card."

"Then we're good to go. Follow me."

Within ten minutes they were checked, sacked, and on their way out of the store. They quickly loaded the groceries into the trunk and got in out of the cold.

Pat shuddered as he started the car and turned up the heater. "You know, that wind is brutal. Why don't we go back to the house and—"

"No, we're not going back to the house until you get clothes for your party. Go to J. C. Penney. It's on Perkins Road, remember?"

Pat sighed. "Yes, I remember."

I'm excited! It's been ages since we've gone shopping.

Tara stifled a groan. Millicent! *Millicent, you will* NOT *go into that dressing room with Uncle Pat and embarrass him. Do you hear me? This is important.*

I hear you. Ice yourself.

It's chill, not ice, Millicent, and you have to promise not to mess with him.

I promise. He's family, after all. I wouldn't do that.

Tara sighed. Thank goodness Uncle Pat couldn't hear this conversation. The rest of the trip to the store was quiet. Pat was concentrating on driving on the still snow-packed roads, and Tara was thinking about Flynn, wondering what he was doing for New Year's Eve. When she got home, she'd call and ask. Maybe he could come over, and they'd bring in the New Year together at her house, while Mona and Uncle Pat were partying elsewhere.

As soon as they reached the store, Tara was all business. She led the way to the men's department. "So, would you rather have slacks and a sports coat or a suit?"

"Not a suit," Pat said.

"Agreed," she said, and began sorting through the racks. "Hold these," she said, and handed him three pairs of slacks, then moved to the other side of the rack and pulled out a couple more before going to the sports coat section.

A clerk quickly approached.

"Hello, I'm David. Would you like me to put these in a changing room for you?"

"Yeah, sure," Pat said, and handed him the slacks, while Tara was sorting through the sports coats. The selection was slim, considering Christmas had just passed, but the good news was that everything was on sale, *because* Christmas had just passed.

"I don't know your arm length, Uncle Pat."

The clerk reappeared, ready to help. "Let me," he said, and whipped out a measuring tape, took a couple of measurements, then began pulling out the ones that would fit.

I like the brown wool. It's the color of chocolate. I loved chocolate. I miss chocolate a lot.

Tara stifled a grin. Millicent.

"For sure try on the brown one, Uncle Pat. There are a couple of pairs of slacks that it would go with."

David, the clerk, smiled an approval. "Your daughter has a

good eye," he said.

Pat looked at Tara and winked. They never bothered to correct their relationship. It was a logical assumption.

Tara chose three more sports coats and handed them over, then watched as Pat followed the clerk into the waiting rooms.

"You have to come out and model them for me," Tara said.

"Okay," he said, his step light as he walked away.

Tara watched him go, thinking she'd never seen him this happy. It made her wonder how much Mona had to do with his willingness to stay in Stillwater, then decided it didn't matter. Whatever it took to stay was fine with her, because her future played into this scenario, too.

Tara loved Flynn. Right now, it felt like she would love him forever. No one knew what the future would bring, but she would like to have a heads up now and then.

"Hey, Millicent?" she whispered.

I'm here.

Tara walked over to a rack of ties and began looking through them so that no one would see her talking to herself. "Is Uncle Pat going to marry Mona O'Mara?"

The future is not set in stone. You know that.

Tara sighed. "Yes, but I would appreciate your best guess."

They would be happy together.

Tara sighed. "And how would this affect me and Flynn?"

The future is not set in stone.

"Dang it, Millicent, I—"

"Hey, Tara, honey, what do you think?"

She turned, and then breath caught in the back of her throat. Uncle Pat was wearing the chocolate sports coat and a pair of black slacks. All of a sudden, she saw her uncle as a stranger would see him, and a lump came in her throat. Her Uncle Pat was handsome.

Her voice shook. "I think you look amazing."

"You think this would be okay for the party?"

"I think it would be perfect," she said, and clutched her fingers to keep them from shaking.

"I'll try on a couple more, but I like this. It all fits."

She nodded, watching as he walked away smiling.

Clothes make the man feel like a man.

"I get it," Tara whispered, then picked up a white shirt and a tie that pulled the outfit together. She knew he wasn't through trying on clothes, but that was the one he would choose. She'd seen a look in his eyes she'd never seen before. Pride was a hard thing to come by, and when it was lost, hard to get back. But she'd seen it just now, and like the clothes he'd been wearing, it looked good on him.

The older she got, the more she cared about her loved ones, living or not so much.

THE CHOCOLATE-brown sports coat and black slacks, along with a new shirt and tie, were hanging in Pat's closet, ready for the party tomorrow night; the groceries were long since put away. Tara's fudge was on the counter, cooling. Her call to Flynn had gone to voicemail, and so she waited impatiently for him to call back.

She moved to the windows, looking out across the street to where Uncle Pat was shoveling off the driveway for the young neighbor whose husband was serving in Afghanistan. The neighbor would have a nice surprise when she got off work and got home tonight.

Pat had a good heart. He deserved some personal happiness. If he and Mona really hit it off, she and Flynn would work the rest of it out. Uncle Pat had sacrificed enough of his life for her. It was time he put some of his needs first.

MARSH STORY popped the top on a beer and picked up his burger.

"Where are the fries? I asked for fries."

Vince shrugged as he chewed. "I don't know. I have mine," he said and dipped another one in ketchup then popped it in his mouth.

Dig was eating a hotdog and Tater Tots. He just shrugged and kept eating.

Marsh sighed. Hooking up with these two had seemed like a good idea at the time, but he wasn't so sure, now. They couldn't even get an order right from the local drive-in. Even though they'd been scoping out their target since a week before Christmas, expecting them to successfully pull off a kidnapping was beginning to look like a mistake.

Marsh looked around the kitchen of May Schulter's home and realized how fortunate for him that she had not been the one to raise him. It was just above the level of pigsty, although to be fair, she'd been in prison now for over three months, which explained the dust, but the hoarder aspect of the place gave him the creeps.

"Weatherman said the snow would start melting tomorrow," Vince offered.

Marsh took a bite of his burger and washed it down with a swig of beer.

"Did you put the truck battery on the charger?"

Vince nodded.

"Good," Marsh said. "So here's the deal. This is Sunday. Stillwater High School resumes classes on Wednesday. We have three days to prepare."

"Prepare for what?" Dig asked. "You said we'd snatch her on her way to school, so we snatch her on her way to school."

Marsh frowned. "We know her uncle leaves for work way before she has to leave the house, and they only have one vehicle, which means she walks."

"Unless she catches a ride. When I was in high school, I used to catch a ride every morning with some of the guys," Vince said.

Marsh's frown deepened. "Then we wait until her uncle leaves the house and take her in a home-invasion-style snatch. That's even better."

Vince squeezed extra ketchup on another french fry and popped it in his mouth. "These fries would be good with jalapeno slices. I like spicy food. We need to try out that Mexico Joe's restaurant while we're here. I'll bet they have some good spicy food."

Marsh snapped and before he thought, slapped Vince on the side of the head. "We're not on vacation! We're here to find the money," he said.

Vince stood up, still holding his burger and still chewing. "Do not hit me again, Marshall. I know the way back home, and I am losing interest by the minute in this crazy scheme of yours."

Dig was shocked by Marsh's behavior. "I'm with Vince. When you first talked about this, I thought you pretty much knew where the money was, and all we were gonna do was dig it up. I didn't count on kidnapping some teenager."

Marshall felt his plan coming undone. He needed their help to get the girl. When he was digging up the money he could dig that hole big enough to bury the both of them, if they kept pissing him off. "Just calm down. Half a million dollars is worth a little trouble, right?"

"Just don't hit me again," Vince muttered.

"I won't. That was my bad. I apologize," Marsh said.

The three men glared at each other in silence as they continued to eat, but the mood was definitely testy. Wednesday would come none too soon.

MONDAY MORNING dawned cold but sunny.

Tara was up before daybreak. By the time Pat was out of the shower and dressed for work, she had a hot breakfast ready.

"Wow, you didn't have to do all this," Pat said, as he sat down to scrambled eggs and sausage.

"I woke early and couldn't go back to sleep. Do you want one slice of toast or two?"

"I'll take two," Pat said. "Aren't you going to eat?"

"I'm good for now," she said. "I ate some sausage while I was cooking it."

"It sure is good," Pat said.

She smiled and put a second piece of bread in the toaster.

A short while later he was gone, and, once again, Tara was on her own. She turned on the television as she swept the floor and then got out Pat's new shirt and ironed all the wrinkles out of it for the party tonight. It was a little bit after eight fifteen when she hung it up then wandered into the living room and sat down to watch TV. She wanted to call Flynn, but not before nine, in case he was sleeping in.

Henry popped up and settled beside her.

He wants to watch the History Channel.

Tara grinned. Millicent always knew what Henry wanted, which was probably why he never talked. "Why?"

We've lived so many past lives we think of it as watching home movies of a family reunion.

Tara blinked. "You're kidding."

No, and this time it's about the French and Indian War, which fits right in with the mood he's been in. That coonskin cap still looks ridiculous.

Tara scanned the TV guide, found the History Channel, and clicked the remote, then sat with them, staring intently at the screen.

We should have popcorn.

Tara frowned. "It's morning. Who eats popcorn in the morning?"

I'll do the popcorn. You stay and watch.

"Seriously? No! Wait! I don't want popcorn."

I saw you. You didn't eat breakfast. It's good fiber. It will be good for your digestive system.

Tara rolled her eyes. "Oh, for the love of God! You did not just suggest I might need a laxative!"

All of a sudden Henry began pointing and then popped up beside the television with his finger on the screen.

Tara leaned forward, staring intently at a painting that supposedly depicted a battle during that time in history.

"Are you saying you were at that battle?"

Henry nodded, then began marching around the couch like he was on guard, then he grabbed his chest and fell backward.

The sudden sound of popcorn popping broke the silence.

"Is that how you died?"

He nodded as he floated toward the ceiling.

Tara felt like crying.

"I'm sorry, Henry. I'm very sorry that you died."

He bounced off a couple of walls to show her that he was fine.

"Okay, I get it. You're happy now, but that was weird, seeing you like that."

Popcorn is done. You should come get it while it's hot.

Tara sighed. There was no way to win an argument with Millicent.

"I'm coming."

IT WAS MID-afternoon when Flynn returned her call, and she could tell by the tone of his voice he was rattled.

"Flynn? What's wrong?"

"I think my dad's been trying to contact me."

Tara sighed. "I wondered when that would start up. Remember, I told you I made a deal with him. I promised that when he was ready, I'd help him talk to you in this life."

"He's never come to you before now?" Flynn asked.

"Nope. Not a peep. Not a sign. What makes you think it's him now?"

"When my phone rings, his name pops up in caller ID, but there's no one there."

Tara could hear the anxiety in Flynn's voice. "I'll help you, but we need to be together to do this. What are you doing for New Year's Eve?"

"Hoping to spend it with you, why?"

"Good. That's why I called you earlier. Mona and Uncle Pat are going to that party. I thought maybe we could ring in the New Year here, unless you have a better idea."

"No parties. I keep hearing too many voices."

"I'll help you with that, too," she said. "Just get here, and we'll see about contacting your dad and blocking the voices."

"Thank you, Moon Girl, more than you can know."

"Can't wait to see you," Tara said.

"I'll bring snacks," he said.

"I made fudge."

"You are my sweet fix. Later."

Tara was still smiling when she disconnected.

TARA TOOK A picture of Pat in all his finery before he left to pick Mona up.

"Have fun, Uncle Pat, but be careful. Drunk drivers and all that, you know."

Pat knew Tara was feeling him out about drinking, which he'd done way too much of in the past. "I've already told Mona I'm the designated driver, so no worries, okay? You and Flynn have fun."

She hugged him. "We will. He's bringing snacks, and there are New Year's Eve shows and movies to watch."

Pat paused and, in a rare gesture of affection, cupped her cheeks and kissed her forehead. "Love you, honey. See you later."

Tara's vision blurred. "Love you, too, Uncle Pat." Moments later, he was gone.

She locked the door, then turned around and caught movement from the corner of her eye.

"Well, there you are," Tara said.

Michael O'Mara's spirit was trying to manifest, and Tara could see he was having trouble gathering energy to do it. "You still haven't crossed over, have you?"

Michael shook his head. *We had a deal.*

"I know that. I haven't gone anywhere. You're the one who didn't make contact."

She felt his frustration, but didn't understand it.

They're here.

She frowned. "Who's here?"

After the money.

Her heart skipped a beat. "Is this why my life is in danger?"

He nodded. *Sorry.*

"OMG. Is this never going to be over? Please! Tell me where it is so the police can recover it, and then that will be that."

He faded. She heard a faint pop, and then he was gone. Tara

was on the verge of panic. "Millicent!"

I'm here. We heard.

"What can I do to make this stop?"

Until you find the money it will never be over.

Tara sat down with a plop, defeated by her lack of control and struggling against the urge to cry. As she sat, she saw a light from outside flash against the curtains. Flynn was here. She wondered if his father's spirit would return, or even if he *could* return.

Flynn was smiling when she opened the door.

"Hey, beautiful," he said softly.

She shivered. "Hey, yourself. I'm really glad you're here."

"So am I," Flynn said. "Some of this stuff needs to go in the fridge."

He handed her the sack of snacks he'd brought, and she headed for the kitchen, dug out the dip and cold drinks and put them in the refrigerator, then turned around to find Flynn had shed his coat and was right behind her.

He opened his arms.

She walked into his embrace and laid her cheek against his chest. When he wrapped his arms around her, she couldn't help but think of how tall he was getting, and how much bigger he was than when they first met. They'd been through a lot together in a few short months, but it was their brush with death that had shifted the focus of their feelings. They'd learned the hard way how swiftly a life could end.

"Tara."

She looked up.

Flynn lowered his head.

She closed her eyes, waiting for it—waiting for the kiss.

His lips were still cool from the chill of the night, but swiftly warmed and softened as the pressure increased, and for Tara, time ceased.

When Flynn finally pulled back, there was a moment when she felt like she'd just lost a piece of herself.

"Oh, wow," Flynn said softly.

"Took the words right out of my mouth," Tara said, and

combed shaky fingers through her hair.

"I think that calls for something cold," Flynn said.

Like a cold shower.

Flynn grinned. "I heard that."

Tara blushed. "OMG. Remembering that you can hear people's thoughts is going to take some readjustment."

He had a defeated look on his face. "Tell me about it. How in the world do you shut out the spirits?"

"I grew up this way, so it seems normal to me. But we obviously need to work on your skills. Do you hear thoughts all the time?"

"It's worse when I let down my guard."

She nodded, thinking of the best way to help him as she got glasses out of the cabinet and filled them with ice. Flynn took the cold drinks out of the refrigerator and opened the dip and chips while she poured their drinks.

"What you're going to have to work on is focus. When you're in a crowd and overwhelmed by the voices, focus specifically on the person you're talking to. Think of it like squinting your eyes against too much sunlight. And until you get better at it, just walk away to center yourself before you go back."

Flynn's eyes widened. "Yeah, okay. I get what you mean. I can do that."

Tara patted his arm. "You'll get it. Let's take the stuff into the living room. You pick out what you want to watch. There are movies on TV or several New Year's Eve parties being broadcast."

"I vote for a movie."

She smiled. "Good choice."

They were on their way to the living room when Flynn's cell phone began to ring. "Oh sorry, I meant to put that on vibrate and forgot." He set down his food, then frowned at the message in the text and held it up for Tara to see. *Call me. Dad.* "This is creepy," Flynn muttered and sat down.

Tara sat down beside him, dipped a corn chip into the dip, and popped it into her mouth. "He was here earlier."

Flynn looked as shocked as he sounded. "What? Why would he come to you?"

Tara sighed. They'd never talked in depth about what she'd gone through with Michael while Flynn was in a coma, because when Flynn woke up, he didn't remember being with his dad, and she hadn't wanted to mention it was his father's spirit that kept him in that condition.

"We made a deal when you were in a coma."

"You and my dad made a deal?"

She nodded. "If he would let you come back—"

"If he would *let* me come back? What the hell, Tara? What exactly was he doing?"

She sighed, swiped a chip in the dip, and put it in his mouth. "Chew. Enjoy. I'll try to explain."

Flynn chewed, but he looked uneasy.

"The simplest explanation is that your dad has unfinished business with you and was trying to talk to you, but you couldn't see or understand him. You just felt the pull of his love."

Flynn was stunned.

Tara kept talking. "He died before he could reveal the location of the money, and he knew that caused you and your mom trouble."

"So that's what he said to you today?"

"Not exactly."

Flynn stilled. "What *exactly* did he say?"

"They're here."

Flynn frowned. "What does that mean?"

"You know those dreams I keep having about dying?"

Flynn's eyes narrowed. "Yes, what about them?"

"There are more people looking for that missing money, and my life is going to be in danger because of it."

Flynn stood up. "No! Damn it, that's enough, Dad! Get your ass here right now and tell us where that money is hidden before you get Tara killed."

Chapter Four

TARA FELT MICHAEL'S spirit coming before she saw him. "He's here," she said.

Flynn was turning in a circle, scanning every corner, looking for substance when substance was long since gone. "Dad! Dad! Where's the money?"

Tara could see Michael trying to manifest, but it wasn't happening. He was little more than a faint shadow that only she could see.

Mona knows.

Tara gasped.

Flynn frowned. "What's wrong?"

"He said your mother knows."

"That's a lie!"

Doesn't know, but she can find.

"Oh . . . okay, he's having trouble making himself understood, Flynn. Don't be mad at him. This is hard. He said she doesn't know, but she can find it. That's a whole other thing. Like if he put it in a place only she would understand."

The shadow swirled, leaving Tara with the impression that she was right on target. But Flynn didn't see it and didn't care. He was angry, and rightly so.

"Then say what has to be said and quit being so secretive. If it wasn't for Tara, I'd be dead. I trust her more than I ever trusted you, and if that hurts, then deal with it."

Tara was torn between wanting to throw herself into Flynn's arms for what he'd said and wanting Michael to spill the beans so this could be over.

I hid it. Tell Mona it's with Aunt Tillie.

Tara nodded. "He said, 'I hid it. Tell Mona it's with Aunt

Tillie.'"

"What does all that mean?" Flynn muttered.

"Maybe your mother will know."

"Oh my God," Flynn said, and began pacing the floor. "Dad! How is this going to help Tara? What if we can't find this in time? Who's after her? Give us a name?"

May . . .

He disappeared.

"Oh. He's gone," Tara said.

"What did he say?"

"He started to say something, but all he got out was the word 'may,' which means nothing."

Flynn took her in his arms. He was so rattled he was shaking. "I'm sorry. I'm so sorry. If something happens to you because of all this I'll never forgive him. You have to tell your cop friends. Maybe they can—"

Tara was as scared as he was, but couldn't let on. Nothing good would come of both of them freaking out.

"We'll talk to your mom, but not tonight. She and Uncle Pat deserve some happiness. Let this night be for them. Come sit down."

"I can't sit," he said.

"Then we'll stand," she said, and made a quick about-face, grabbed her iPod, scanned the titles, selected, then set it on the speaker.

Slow country music filled the room. Flynn looked at her, then sighed and opened his arms.

Tara walked into them, smiling as she looked up. "The last time we danced together was out at Boomer Lake on that old pier, remember?"

"I remember everything about you," he said softly.

He swept her into a quick turn and began slow-dancing her between the sofa and the television, then behind it and into the kitchen, then out and down the hall into the shadows—still dancing, still in each other's arms.

It was the best night of Tara's life, but if Michael O'Mara

didn't come through for them, it could very easily become the last night. Living on the edge wasn't living. It was waiting to die.

Millicent and Henry were sitting on the back of the sofa, watching the two young lovers. There was no need for words. They'd known this day would come. Their baby was growing up. They just needed to get her over this latest hurdle safely so she could continue the trip.

IT WAS FIFTEEN minutes to midnight when Flynn woke up with his fingers tangled in Tara's hair. The television show they'd been watching was obviously over, and the program was showing a huge crowd down at Bricktown, in downtown Oklahoma City. The camera was on a big shiny ball, and the countdown to midnight was on. The last thing he remembered was watching The Flaming Lips performing onstage at the Zoo Amphitheatre. It appeared he wasn't the only one who'd zonked out. Tara was stretched out on the sofa with her head in his lap, sound asleep. She'd become important to him in ways he would never have imagined. She wasn't just his girlfriend anymore. She was the sail that kept him on a steady course.

He glanced at the clock. Not long until midnight. He untangled his fingers from her hair and then rubbed the back of his finger down her cheek.

"Wake up, Moon Girl. It's almost midnight."

Tara took a slow breath and then opened her eyes, groaning as she pushed herself upright. "I went to sleep. I'm sorry."

"Don't be. I did, too. It's almost midnight," he said, pointing at the clock.

"Oh! Oh, my gosh!" she said, and jumped up. "Wait. I've got to brush my hair and—"

He was laughing as he stood up and stretched. "You need to brush your hair to see in the New Year?"

"It's a girl thing," she said, and dashed down the hall to the bathroom.

Flynn was still smiling as he walked into the kitchen. He got a cold pop out of the refrigerator, two glasses out of the cabinet, and divided up the drink. It wasn't champagne, but then they weren't twenty-one, either.

Tara came back into the kitchen with the tangles gone and a smile on her face.

Breath caught in the back of Flynn's throat as he watched her walking toward him. She was all long legs in tight jeans and a body that filled out that white sweatshirt just fine.

Without thinking, he tuned into her thoughts and tuned out just as quickly before someone made a move into a place neither one was ready to go. He handed over one of the glasses.

"It's not champagne, but it's legal."

She smiled as she took a sip. "It's bubbly. It tickled my nose. It's perfect."

They lifted their glasses.

"To us," Flynn said.

They took a quick drink then looked through the doorway to the television in the next room. They could hear the crowd counting down the seconds.

Five.

Four.

Three.

Two.

One.

Flynn took the glass out of Tara's hands and set it on the counter, then took her in his arms.

"Happy New Year, Tara Luna."

"Happy New Year, Flynn O'Mara."

That kiss was seventeen years in the making and the culmination of every dream a young girl might have had of happily ever after.

And when it was finally over, they didn't speak or move; standing cheek to cheek in an embrace while every thought they had was playing live and in color in each other's head.

It was nearly an hour later before Pat came home from the party. Flynn was long gone and Tara was in her room asleep. He peeked in to reassure himself she was okay, and then got ready for bed, happy that tomorrow was a holiday and a day to sleep in. He had no idea that Tara's life was in danger, or that Flynn would wind up in a race against time to save her.

TARA HAD BEEN dozing, waiting for her uncle to get home. It wasn't until she heard his key in the door, and then the familiar sound of his footsteps that she relaxed her vigilance and went to sleep.

The feathers tied to the dream catcher on the wall above her bed shifted slightly as Millicent slipped past to settle onto the bed with Tara. She had often slept beside her when Tara was little and having bad dreams, wrapping her in ethereal arms and cradling her as best she could. She hadn't done it in years, but her fear for Tara's safety had drawn her back to old habits.

Henry had traded his coonskin cap for a suit of armor and a sword and stood silently in a corner, watching the doorway. If an intruder came, he was ready to defend his girl.

Pat snored softly in his bed without dreaming, unaware the residents in the house were preparing for a war.

When they woke the next morning, none of them could have known they were on the verge of the greatest battle they would ever face. Not even Tara, who saw ghosts and spoke to spirits, could see into her own future. All she felt was an impending doom without a timeline to track it, so she made pancakes for breakfast because they were her favorite, trying not to think of it as a last meal.

IT WAS NEW Year's Day.

Marsh stared at a map of the city of Stillwater. The little house on Duck Street, where Pat Carmichael lived with his niece, Tara Luna, was circled in red. He had three different escape routes marked on the map, all of which would eventually get them out of town and back here to May's house. After reading of all of the teenager's exploits in the aftermath of the tornado that had hit the city last fall, he was convinced that all she had to do was tune in to the money's location and tell them where to dig. He knew just enough to be dangerous, if she wouldn't cooperate.

Tomorrow, Tara's school would resume. Marsh and his assistants would be stationed at the end of the block on her street, watching for the uncle to leave for work. Once he was gone, they'd grab her and run. No one would even know she was missing until long after school began, and even then, it shouldn't be a cause for alarm. Lots of teenagers skipped school. He certainly had in his day. Why would she be any different?

PAT WAS SOPPING up pancakes with great abandon while talking about the party from the night before. "I met this guy who works out at the country club. Really nice fellow. His wife is a teacher at one of the elementary schools."

Tara listened as she smeared another pat of butter on the hot stack on her plate, while Pat kept talking.

"Mona said she went to school with his wife at Ripley. Have we ever been to Ripley? It's not far from here, but Mona said, as a town, there's not much left there anymore."

Tara reached for the syrup and poured some on her pancakes, then sat down and took her first bite. The pancakes were light and fluffy, and there was still butter on the bite that hadn't melted. That first bite was always her favorite. She *uhmmed* in pleasure.

Pat looked up at her and smiled.

"These are delicious, honey. You're a good cook. I don't think I say that enough, but you are. You have your mother's touch. She could make anything taste good, even when there wasn't much to work with."

Tara smiled. She liked it when Uncle Pat mentioned her mother like this. It made her feel connected, even though she didn't have a single memory of her parents' existence. She continued to eat as Pat talked more about the party.

"They had a live band that played everything from 'Boogie Woogie Bugle Boy' to 'Who Let The Dogs Out,' and by the way,

Mona sure can dance. I had to go some to keep up with her."

Tara eyed her uncle, trying to imagine him sweeping Mona around a dance floor. "Did she like your new outfit?"

Pat smirked a little. "She said I was handsome, so I guess the answer is yes."

"You *are* handsome, Uncle Pat."

He shrugged. "When I was younger, girls used to say I looked a little bit like Sean Connery. 'Course, young people these days don't even know who that is, but he was 'the' James Bond in my day."

She smiled. He used to say that a lot when she was little, and then he'd sort of let go of that happy part of his life. It was good to know he was back in that mindset again.

"So, are you and Mona getting serious?"

He frowned. "We're dating." Then he changed the subject. "Did you and Flynn have a good time last night?"

Tara nodded, unaware she had a dreamy expression on her face he didn't much like.

"We did. We ate the snacks he brought and some of the fudge I made. We even danced a little bit and then fell asleep on the sofa watching TV and almost missed seeing in the New Year."

Pat wanted to say more, but didn't. Tara was only a couple of months shy of eighteen, which was legal age. She'd never given him a day of trouble in the boy department, and he wasn't going to start pushing his weight around now. Besides, he liked Flynn and, for now, that was enough.

"So what do you want to do today?" he asked.

She shrugged. "The snow is melting, but Nikki is still sick. Flynn and his mom are going out of town to a family dinner today. I think I'd just as soon stay home. Besides, the Oklahoma State Cowboys are playing in a bowl game this afternoon, and we'll want to watch that. I might go for a walk later just to get out of the house, but that's as far as I'd want to go."

"Good. So it's settled. By any chance, is there enough batter for another stack of pancakes?"

She nodded and started to get up to make them, but Pat

waved her off.

"You keep eating. I've got this."

She poured some more syrup on her pancakes and dug in while he used up the last of the batter. The day was starting out in a good way.

TARA MADE sandwiches and snack foods near noon and put them all in the refrigerator. Still full of pancakes, neither one of them wanted lunch and decided to wait until mid-afternoon and eat during the bowl game. With a couple of hours before it began, Tara was ready to get out of the house. She had on a pair of old jeans, a blue sweatshirt, and had her hair tied back at the nape of her neck. She bundled up in her heavy coat and went to the front closet to get her old cowboy boots and gloves. The sun was out and slowly melting the snow, but it was still cold. When Pat saw her carrying her boots to the front door, he spoke up.

"Hey honey, if you want to go somewhere, I'll take you."

"I'm not going anywhere in particular. I'm just going for a walk. I have my phone. I'll be fine."

"Do you have gloves?"

"In my pocket."

"Okay, but don't stay gone too long, and if you freeze out, give me a call and I'll come get you."

She nodded. "And if you get hungry before I get back, there's food in the fridge."

He waved.

She slipped out the door and put on her gloves as she started down the steps. The cold air was like a slap in the face to the blah feeling she'd been having. This was just what she needed.

The crust on the top of the snow made crunching sounds as she walked toward the street. A part of her wanted to run through the pristine white, throw herself down on her back, and make angels in the snow like when she was little. But knowing she'd have snow in her hair and down her neck, never mind the wet clothing, dampened the urge. Rational thinking prevailed.

When she got to the sidewalk, she turned left, heading toward the university. It was exciting to know that this time next year she'd be a student at OSU. She had no idea what her course of study might be, but had a couple of years to figure that out.

About four blocks from home, a car turned the corner and came down the street toward her. She recognized Davis Breedlove and Bethany Fanning. She'd had a rocky start with the two when she first started school here. Making friends with the head cheerleader at Stillwater High School and the quarterback of the football team had not been on her wish list. But life, circumstance, and Tara's psychic abilities had saved Bethany from dying at the hands of an abductor.

Davis braked and rolled down a window.

"Hey, Tara! Need a ride?"

"No, I'm just out for a walk, but thank you!"

They smiled and drove on.

Her steps felt lighter. She had friends, good friends, something she'd never had before she and Uncle Pat moved here.

A few blocks later, she found herself walking on campus. It would be a couple of weeks before a new semester would begin, so it was nearly absent of students, but the vibes were still there—hopes and dreams of so many futures. She wanted to be a part of that.

She was just about to head back when she saw a man come out of a building up ahead and realized it was Nate Pierce, the assistant professor of geology. Their lives had already crossed twice in the short time she and Pat had lived in Stillwater, and she considered him a friend. The dream catcher over her bed was a gift from him and his family.

When he saw her, he looked surprised and then smiled and headed toward her.

"Hello! Are you lost?"

She laughed. "No, just out for a walk. I bet you're on your way somewhere to watch the bowl game."

He laughed, his dark eyes twinkling. "Guilty. I'm meeting some friends at Eskimo Joe's, which guarantees it will be a loud and noisy game."

Tara smiled.

Nate eyed her carefully. There was something different about her today. "Is everything okay? You seem . . . quieter."

She shrugged. "I'm fine. Just dealing with some personal stuff."

He frowned. "If there is anything I can do, you have only to ask. You saved my niece's life. It would be my honor to return a favor."

Tara shook her head. "I'm fine, and you better get going, or you'll miss kick-off. I'm heading home myself."

"Want a ride?"

"No. I'm good, but thank you, Nate."

He started to leave and then stopped, feeling a concern that seemed out of place. "Are you sure?"

"I'm sure," she said, and walked away.

The sun was halfway between zenith and the western horizon when Tara turned and headed for home. She was starting to get hungry and thought of the sandwiches and dip she'd made for game time. She was smiling to herself, certain that Uncle Pat was most likely already digging in. She took out her cell phone and hit speed dial to call home.

Pat answered on the second ring. She could hear the roar of the television and the pre-game banter of the announcers.

"Hey, Uncle Pat, it's me."

"Hi, sugar. Are you on your way home?"

"Yes. I'll be there in about fifteen minutes."

"Don't you want me to come get you?"

"No. You'll miss kick-off. Just save me some food. I'm starving."

He laughed. "Deal. See you soon."

"Love you."

As soon as the words came out of her mouth, the hair stood up on the back of her neck. Why did that feel like goodbye instead of a gesture of affection?

"Love you, too, honey. Hurry home."

She disconnected, dropped her phone in her pocket and increased the length of her stride. All of a sudden, the urge to get home was overwhelming. She looked behind her, but there was no one there. Not a car in sight, or a person on either side of the street. She told herself she was just being silly, but kept moving, anxious to get within the four walls of home.

Chapter Five

MARSH AND VINCE had come to town purposefully to scope out the different streets they could use for escape routes should the need arise. They'd already driven past the target house on Duck Street and were about fifteen blocks away when Vince suddenly pointed at a tall, dark-haired girl walking toward them on the sidewalk.

"Hey! Isn't that her? Isn't that Tara Luna?"

Marsh's heart skipped a beat. It *was* her, and the fact that she was out here all alone, and there wasn't another car in sight, seemed like an omen.

"Yes, that's her," Marsh said.

"What are we gonna do?" Vince asked.

"Shut up and let me think," Marsh said, and drove past without looking at her.

The moment he reached the end of the second block, he made a U-turn in the street and backtracked. This was too good an opportunity to ignore. They were coming up fast behind her as he threw the Taser into Vince's lap.

"When I hit the brakes, you get out and shoot her with this. I'll grab her, toss her on the floorboard, and we're out of here."

"What if someone sees us?"

"Look around. It's cold. Drapes are drawn across windows. That football game is starting that everyone has been talking about. No one will be looking out a window."

"Oh, man," Vince muttered, and grabbed the Taser. He knew how to use it, but he'd never used it on a person before.

Marsh gunned the engine. Vince's hand was on the door handle. They were less than a dozen feet behind her when Marsh hit the brakes. Vince jumped out on the run just as Tara spun.

He caught a glimpse of a pretty girl with a very frightened expression on her face. As she turned to run, he pulled the trigger.

TARA SAW THE old black pickup as it passed her, but thought nothing of it. When her cell phone rang, and she saw it was Flynn, the pickup was quickly forgotten.

"Hey, Flynn."

"Hey, honey, I meant to call before kickoff, and now it's about to happen. I knew you'd be glued to the set so I thought I'd better talk fast."

She laughed. "I'm not even home. I got sick of being in the house and went for a walk. I'm already on the way home though. I have to hurry, or Uncle Pat will eat all the good stuff I made."

Flynn's chuckle rolled through her like warm water on snow, melting her from the inside out.

"Are you having a good time at your aunt and uncle's house?" she asked.

"Yeah, but more important, so's Mom. She's had a hard time dealing with all that's happened. You know how parents are—they're either on a guilt trip, or laying one on you." Then the moment he said it, he sighed. "My bad. You don't know that, do you, Moon Girl?"

"I have a parent. Although he's my uncle, it doesn't change the parent aspect, and I get it. Don't go apologizing for—"

Millicent's voice was suddenly screaming in her ear. *Run, Tara run!*

She heard tires screeching on the street behind her and spun around, thinking someone was about to have a wreck. Instead, she saw a man jump out of the same black truck that had just passed her a few moments earlier, and he was running toward her. Her heart dropped. It was happening!

"Help! Flynn! It's happening," she screamed, and turned to run, felt a sharp pain in the back of her thigh and dropped into the snow, unable to move or talk, shaking convulsively from the Taser's electrodes.

Flynn heard the tires, her cry for help and the warning, then nothing. She was being abducted! Why wasn't she running? Why was she suddenly silent? Why wasn't he picking up on her thoughts anymore? God in heaven, what had they done to her?

His heart was hammering so hard against his chest that he thought he'd pass out, but he knew exactly what was happening. Her nightmare was coming true, and he was too far away to help.

He was about to hang up and call Pat and the police when he realized he could hear men's voices. She must have dropped her phone, and the line was still open. He held his breath, listening intently to everything they were saying, praying he would hear a name or recognize a voice.

"GRAB HER!" Marsh said.

"I downed her. You're the big shot. You grab her."

"Damn it, Vince, at least get her feet. We don't have all day here."

Vince yanked the electrodes out of her leg, pocketed the Taser, and did as he was told. But the moment they put their hands on her, they were enveloped in a swirling wind of cold and snow. It blistered their skin and eyeballs so fast they nearly dropped her.

"What's happening? What the hell's happening?" Marsh yelled.

"Stop talking! Hurry up and open the damn door," Vince shouted, squinting against the blast of ice crystals slicing his face.

Within seconds they had her in the truck, took off with a screech of tires, took a right at the next block, and disappeared down an alley.

It took exactly fifteen seconds—a far easier snatch than they could ever have imagined. By the time they cleared the city limits without a cop car in sight, they were laughing hysterically.

"We're half-way to more money than we've ever had before," Marsh said. "The rest is up to her."

FLYNN LISTENED until he heard car doors slamming and the

sounds of an engine disappearing, and then he was running, yelling at his mom as he went.

Mona came running from the kitchen. "Flynn! What on earth?"

"Tara has been kidnapped. Call Pat. I'm calling the police."

Mona gasped. "How do you know this?"

"I was talking to her when it happened! I heard her scream once and then nothing. I heard them talking after they grabbed her. Hurry! Tell him the police will be at his house soon, and that I know why it happened. Tell him we're on our way home."

"Oh, dear God!" Mona cried.

Ignoring the shocked looks on her family's faces, she ran for her cell phone as Flynn stepped outside to make the call to the police.

Unlike Tara, he did not have the Stillwater Police Department on speed dial and took a few moments to pull up the info. As soon as he got the number, he made the call and waited for it to be answered.

"Stillwater Police Department."

He was talking fast, his voice shaking in an effort to get it all said.

"I need to report a kidnapping, and you need to contact Detectives Rutherford and Allen. It has to do with a case they worked."

And so it began. Questions as to how he knew and what he heard, and then even more questions.

"Look. My mom and I are out of town. You have all my information. It will take about forty-five minutes to get home. As soon as I get back to Stillwater I'll help the detectives any way I can. In the meantime, contact her uncle, Pat Carmichael. He might have known more about her location when it happened."

IT WAS TWO minutes after kick-off when Pat's phone rang. His delight in hearing Mona's voice ended the moment she started talking. He couldn't believe—wouldn't believe—and was arguing until she screamed his name.

"Pat! Stop! How do I know? I know because Flynn was talking to her when it happened! He heard her scream. He heard the kidnappers talking. He said to tell you to stay home, that the police will be there within minutes. We're on the way home and will be there within the hour. I'm sorry. I'm so sorry, but I'll be there soon. You're not going through this alone."

Pat's heart was hammering so hard he couldn't breathe. His worst fear had just been realized. The very thing that set her apart from normal people also made her a target. As soon as Mona hung up, he tried to call Tara. It rang and rang and then went to voicemail.

Breath caught in the back of his throat as he jumped up from the sofa. By the time he ran out onto the porch he was sobbing. This had to be a mistake. Any second she would appear, see him standing out on the porch and wave. But he couldn't see the end of the porch for the tears and staggered back into the house to get his coat. He didn't care what Flynn said about waiting for the cops. She was his life, and some creep had snatched her. It didn't matter why they took her. He was going to get her back.

He had his coat on and was heading out the door when a police cruiser pulled up into the drive. When an unmarked car pulled up beside it and he saw Detective Rutherford getting out, his legs went out from under him. He sat down on the steps to keep from falling.

TARA WAS TRYING to focus, but her body was in too much pain and shock. She tried to think Flynn's name in the hopes that he would 'hear' her, but her mind was blank. She could feel saliva running out of the corner of her mouth, and her heart was racing too fast. She tried to scream, but her jaw was locked; her teeth clenched together so tightly she couldn't open her mouth enough to form a word. They'd tossed her inside the pickup like an unwanted backpack and fastened her hands and feet together with duct tape. The two men were talking as if she wasn't even there, verbally patting themselves on the back at how easy it had been. When she finally got a good look at the driver, it was a visual punch in the gut. It was the man from her dream—the man with the pockmarked face. Her nightmare was coming true.

She tried to scream again, but nothing came out but a moan. If she could only move, the driver's knee was within kicking distance of her foot. But before she could take another breath, the truck tires that had been humming along the highway suddenly fell off onto a rougher surface. She could hear the wheels spinning, trying to gain traction in the melting snow.

They were no longer on a highway! Where in God's name were they taking her? She needed to sit up, to at least see where they were going so she could send a message to Flynn, but the two men were still talking as if she wasn't even there, and all she could see was the underside of the dashboard.

The driver suddenly cursed, and before Tara could brace herself, the truck fell off into a pothole. The jolt bounced Tara upward, slamming her forehead against the underside of the dash, knocking her unconscious.

The next thing she knew, someone was wiping her face with a cold rag. She opened her eyes, saw a room straight out of a TV episode of a reality show about hoarding, and this time the scream came up her throat live and in color.

DIG WAS HOLDING a snow-packed rag on the knot on Tara's forehead and unprepared for her return to consciousness. When she screamed, he stumbled backward and would have fallen flat on his backside but for Vince. And no matter what he did or said, the bitch just kept screaming.

Marsh came flying into the room, his clothes awry and his hair standing up on top of his head like he'd been running his fingers over and over through the greasy strands.

"Shut it, girl! We're miles from nowhere, and no one can hear you scream," he yelled.

All of a sudden doors began opening and closing, and pictures hanging on the wall hit the floor, shattering the glass into thousands of tiny pieces. Boxes stacked against the wall on the other side of the room began to tumble, and the trash that had been loose was now flying through the air, creating a maelstrom from the debris.

Dig screamed and started running for the door, but it wouldn't open.

"It's her! She's making it happen!" Marsh shouted and ran toward Tara, yanked her up from the sofa where she was lying, and slapped her so hard her nose began to bleed. "Stop it! Stop it now, or I'll take a knife to your face!"

To prove his point, he popped his switchblade and jabbed it against her cheek.

Tara moaned and reached for her nose, swiping at the blood with the back of her hand. "Stop, Millicent! Stop!" she cried.

The paper in the air dropped to the floor. The silence was almost as frightening as the chaos had been.

"Who's Millicent?" Vince cried.

Tara shuddered as Marsh pushed the tip of the knife a little bit deeper into her cheek. Any more pressure, and it would cut her. "You can kill me. I can't stop you. But you sign your own death warrants if you do. Millicent will peel the skin off your bodies and hang you from the rafters."

Oooh, good one, Tara. If only I could, it would already be done.

Marsh's eyes widened. "Who's Millicent?"

"One of my ghosts."

Marsh's hand was suddenly trembling as he moved the knife from her cheek. "Your ghost?"

"I have two," Tara said. "They're always with me. Always."

Vince moaned. "Why didn't we know this ahead of time? I'm done. I want out of this. Now."

Marsh waved the knife at Vince. "It's too late for all that." He turned and glared at Tara. "You do a favor for us, and when we get what we came for, we'll let you go."

No, they won't.

I know that. Find Flynn and tell him.

He can't hear us. He hears only the living. You have to tell him where you are.

But I don't know where I am.

This house is a long way from the city. There is no number, no name on a road, no name on the mailbox. I will find a way to help you.

Don't leave me!

Henry is here. Stay strong. I will be back.

Tara stifled a sob and made herself focus on what the men were saying.

"What favor do you want?" she asked.

"Tell us where Michael O'Mara hid the drug money, and we're gone."

"Michael O'Mara is dead, and I don't know where he hid the drug money."

Marsh grinned. "But that's why you're here. You can talk to the dead. Just ask him."

"I can't call up the dead. I don't go to them. It doesn't work that way. If they need something, sometimes they come to me, but O'Mara is a spirit who has no reason to tell me anything, so he won't."

Vince moaned. "This is wrong. We shouldn't be messing around trying to conjure up spirits and make ghosts angry. What if they follow us home?"

Marsh looked nervous.

Dig started to cry.

Marsh spun toward Dig to shut him up and accidentally knocked over a small mountain of trash bags. They fell over onto Tara and Vince, who promptly disappeared from view.

FLYNN WAS SICK, staring blindly at the scenery flashing by as his mother sped down the highway toward home. He kept trying to lock into Tara's thoughts, but it was as if she had vanished. Either she was unconscious or already dead. He wouldn't let himself believe they would just kill her without trying to find the money first. It made no sense.

He was so angry at his father. Every bit of what they had gone through, and were going through again, was because of him and that drug money. He glanced at his mother, but her jaw was set and her eyes fixed on the road before them. He didn't want to upset her any more than she already was. Like him, she felt guilty that it was her ex-husband who'd started all this mess.

His cell phone rang. It was Detective Rutherford.

"Hello?"

"Hey kid, it's me, Rutherford. We found where they snatched her. Her phone was still there. We're canvassing the area and have gotten similar comments from a couple of the neighbors. By any chance, do you know anyone who drives an old black truck? They think maybe a Dodge. It was loaded with firewood."

Flynn ran through the names of people he knew, and none of them drove a vehicle like that.

"No, I don't. Is that what the kidnappers were driving?"

"We're not sure. But we have reports of it in the area this morning, as well as several days prior and always with the same load of wood. How far are you from Stillwater?"

"About twenty minutes."

"Come straight to Tara's house."

"Yes, sir. See you soon."

He dropped the phone back in his pocket.

"Who was that?" his mother asked.

"Detective Rutherford. They found Tara's phone and where she was snatched. Asked me if I knew anyone who drove an old black Dodge with a load of firewood in the back."

"Do you?"

"No. Does it sound familiar to you?"

She shook her head. "I can't wait to get to Pat. He's bound to be a wreck. That girl is his life."

Flynn didn't comment, but Tara Luna was the beginning and end of his world, as well. He couldn't imagine a life without her in it. His eyes narrowed angrily as he stared out through the windshield, trying to figure out the best way to begin this conversation with his mother. He had put it off, but now was the opportune time to talk when they would not be interrupted.

"Mom, I need to tell you something and ask you something."

She gave him a nervous glance and then kept her eyes on the road. "Like what?"

"Dad's spirit came to try and tell me something last night while I was at Tara's."

She flinched as if he'd slapped her. "I don't like this. He needs to go away and leave you alone."

"Actually, he came to warn Tara that there were other people after her because of that missing money, but his energy is weak, and he couldn't tell her much."

"Oh my God! That money is going to be the death of all of us before it's recovered."

"Which brings me to the thing I need to ask you. Dad said you would know where it was."

She gasped. "That's a lie! I have no idea—"

"No. I said that wrong. Tara and I think he was trying to say that he hid it where only you would understand the clues he gave her."

She frowned. "What kind of clues?"

"He said to tell you it's with Aunt Tillie."

Mona jumped. "Oh, dear lord! Yes, I do know what that means. What do we do?"

"Tell the detectives everything you know and let them worry about it."

"Yes, of course. It just startled me so bad I wasn't thinking."

"Who's Aunt Tillie?" Flynn asked.

"An old woman who lived in the house behind us when we were first married."

"Do you know where she is now? What if she moved?"

Mona shook her head. "She definitely moved on, but I know where to find her."

Flynn waited, but cryptically, she said nothing more.

MARSH AND DIG were throwing boxes and trash bags out into the yard with wild abandon, trying to get to Vince and Tara, who were at the bottom of the pile.

"Hurry, Dig, hurry!" Marsh cried. "They'll suffocate if we don't get them out."

Dig was madly throwing things behind him, kicking aside boxes and carrying the other stuff out into the back yard and giving it a toss.

"It probably killed them both," Dig muttered, as he dragged another trash bag off the pile.

"There's Vince's arm!" Marsh said. "Get those boxes off his shoulder!"

"And there's the girl!" Dig said, pointing to a hand just visible in a space near Marsh's foot.

Now that their targets had been located, it was easier to uncover them. Vince had taken the brunt of the load and was lying halfway across Tara's body. Marsh dropped to his knee to check for pulses, and when he felt them both, leaned back with a relieved sigh.

"They're alive. Here, help me move Vince first."

They dragged Vince's body over onto his back, then propped him up against some trash bags before they went back for the girl. Marsh felt for the pulse in her neck. It was steady, but she was far too still. This was the second time in less than an hour she'd been knocked unconscious. If she didn't have a concussion before, she was bound to now. He groaned. None of this was going as planned. They should have waited until tomorrow and been more prepared, but it was too late to take back.

Except for the blood streaked across her cheek from where he'd slapped her in the nose, she was white as a sheet. He patted her cheek lightly, trying to wake her up.

"Tara! Tara Luna! Wake up!"

But she didn't so much as blink.

He cursed. They had her, but there was no telling how long it would be before they could use her. If she didn't wake up, their whole plan was a bust.

"Dig, help me carry her to my bed," he said.

Dig got her feet as Marsh slid his hands beneath her armpits. Together, they lifted her up and made their way through the path of debris to the only room left in the house that wasn't completely full of junk.

"Put her on the bed," Marsh said, "then bring me a clean rag and a pan of snow."

"What about Vince?" Dig asked.

Marsh sighed. "Put a cold compress on his head. He'll either wake up or he won't."

"Oh, man," Dig muttered, and ran to do the boss's bidding.

TARA WAS STANDING on a precipice. Infinity was before her, but everyone she loved was behind her. She wouldn't move for fear she'd fall.

Go back, girl. You don't belong here.

Tara turned. Michael O'Mara was behind her.

You're the one who put me here. Show me the way to go home.

He pointed, and her focus shifted to two spirits standing in a veil of swirling mist.

They'll take you. Go. Hurry.

What about the money? I need to know where it is so I can go home.

When you know where it is, they will kill you.

Tara moaned. They're going to kill me anyway. I saw it happen in my sleep.

Fate can change. First go back.

All of a sudden the two other spirits had enveloped her. She had the sensation of being cradled and someone whispering in her ear.

TARA GASPED. HER eyes flew open. The man with the pockmarked face was sitting on the bed beside her, and for some reason, her face was wet and freezing.

"What? Stop . . . don't touch me," she mumbled, and began pushing at his hands.

Marsh stood up and dropped the rag full of snow-melt into the basin. "So, you woke up."

"My head . . . what happened?"

"Shit fell on you. Sorry. It appears Mother dear was a hoarder."

Her head was swimming, and she was still trying to make sense of what happened when what he said finally sank in.

"Mother who?"

"It doesn't matter. Shut up and let me think."

Tara sighed and closed her eyes.

To Marsh's dismay, she was unconscious again. Definitely a concussion. They were going to have to keep waking her up at intervals or take a chance on her not waking up at all.

"Damn it all to hell," he muttered, and got up to go check on Vince.

FLYNN AND MONA reached Pat's house in record time, but there were so many police cars there, they had to park at the curb. He got out on the run, leaving his mother to follow. The policeman standing on the porch started to stop him until someone inside the house yelled,"Let him pass."

Flynn burst into the room, his heart pounding, frantically searching for a positive sign on someone's face. It didn't happen. Rutherford looked like Flynn felt, and Pat was unashamedly crying.

Mona came in and went straight to Pat's side.

"Talk to me," Rutherford said. "Tell me again, from the start, what you heard."

It's all Flynn had been thinking about. He began counting off the clues in order. "We were talking. I heard brakes screeching. Tara screamed my name and said, 'It's happening.' After that, I heard nothing. I was about to hang up and call the police when I realized she must have dropped her phone in the snow, and the line was still open. I could hear two men talking. The names I heard were Vince and Marsh. I don't know how they silenced her, but it was sudden and I can't pick up—"

He caught himself. No one but Tara knew he could hear people's thoughts, and now was not the time to reveal it. "I couldn't make out anything else they said. When I heard them rev the engine and take off, I knew she was gone."

Rutherford pointed at Flynn. "What did she mean by 'it's

happening'?"

Flynn glanced at Pat, sorry that Tara had shared this with him and not her uncle. "She's been having nightmares of a man with a pockmarked face strangling her. She kept saying that she died."

Mona squeezed Pat's hand.

"Sometimes fate can be changed with forewarning," Pat muttered. "That's what my mother and sister always said. I will not believe she's dead."

"Do you know why they took her?" Rutherford asked.

He nodded. "She said it had to do with that missing drug money my father was supposed to have buried."

Rutherford slapped the side of his leg in frustration. "Everyone connected to that is either dead or in prison! What are we missing?"

Flynn shrugged. "I don't know. I just know that's what she said."

Mona was about to bring up the subject of the missing money when all of a sudden the air in the room was so cold their breath was coming out in tiny clouds.

Allen was still freaked about what Millicent had done to him when he was alone in the car, and now being in this house again made it worse. He bolted up from his chair.

"What's happening?" he cried.

Flynn could feel the energy. He would bet his life it was one or both of Tara's ghosts, and when a stack of magazines fell off a table by the front window and landed on the floor with a loud splat, he knew it.

Everyone turned toward the sound and then stared in growing horror as the curtains at the windows moved aside on their own, revealing the windowpanes.

At first Flynn saw nothing, and then he realized a word was beginning to appear on one of the windows that had fogged over.

"Look!" he cried. "The ghosts are trying to tell us something!"

Pat pushed his way to the window, watching intently as one

letter after another appeared.

First the *M*, then an *A*, then a *Y*.

Flynn's heart skipped a beat. *May* was the last word his dad said the other day before he disappeared. What did it mean?

"May! What does *may* mean?" Rutherford asked.

"Wait! There's more!" Flynn said, pointing to the next letter appearing below the first word.

First an *S*, then a *C*, then an *H*.

When the *U* appeared, Rutherford grunted. "If an *L* comes next, I got it."

Sure enough, the next letter was an *L*. The *T*, *E*, and *R* were after the fact.

"May Schulter!" Rutherford muttered. "What does she have to do with this? I thought we had everyone connected to that gang behind bars! What the hell are we missing?"

And just like that, the cold air was gone.

"Message delivered," Flynn said softly. *Talk to me, Moon Girl. For God's sake, wake up and talk to me.*

The silence was killing him.

"We're going to the station," Rutherford said. "We need to go back through our records and see what or who we can find with a connection to Schulter."

Flynn knew his mother had yet to reveal what she knew about the missing money, but now was probably not the time.

"I want to go with you," Flynn said.

Rutherford frowned. "There's nothing you can—"

Flynn shook his head. "Please. I'll explain on the way."

Rutherford shrugged. "Go get in the car, kid."

Flynn glanced at his mother. She hesitated then nodded. Moments later he was out the door and in the back seat of their car.

Rutherford got in behind the wheel. Allen slid into the passenger seat beside him, and then both of them turned and gave Flynn a look.

"What do you know that we don't?" Rutherford asked.

"Remember when I was in that coma?"

Allen frowned. "Yeah, but what does that have to do

with—"

"I came back with a skill I didn't have before."

Rutherford's eyes widened. "Can you see ghosts, too?"

"No. I have no connection to the dead, but I can hear the thoughts of people who are alive."

Allen snorted softly. "You are so—"

"The first thought you had was bullshit, and now you're thinking to yourself not to think about the fact that you haven't qualified on the gun range lately."

Allen gasped.

Rutherford's mouth opened, but before he could talk, Flynn turned it on him.

"You're thinking to yourself that I would make a hell of a cop with a skill like that, and how can you talk me into law enforcement after I graduate."

Rutherford grinned. "Word for, hot damn, excuse my French, word. Now let's get to the station. We've got to find our girl."

Chapter Six

TARA WOKE UP off and on throughout the evening, each time to the horrified realization this wasn't the nightmare—it was real. Once she saw a rat looking down at her from a stack of boxes, but her head throbbed so badly she wasn't sure if that was a hallucination or if it was actually happening.

Another time she felt tiny wings fluttering against her cheeks and woke up to a cockroach running across her cheek. She slapped it off with a groan of disgust and tried to get up, but the room was spinning, so she shifted focus to trying to contact Flynn, but her thoughts were in free fall. She knew she had a concussion. What she didn't know was what would happen to her if she didn't get medical help. It was all so frightening—not knowing when or why they would kill her—only that it was so.

She felt Millicent's presence, but couldn't hear her. That scared her worse than not being able to hear Flynn. She couldn't even see Henry. Every aspect of her paranormal skills was gone. All she could do was pray that the blows to her head were responsible, and when she was no longer concussed, they would come back.

The third time she woke up it was dark, and they'd taped her wrists and ankles back together. She moaned, crying out in a weak, shaky voice.

"Someone? Anyone? I need to use the bathroom."

She heard feet shuffling, and then Marsh walked into the room and turned on the light.

"What's your name?" he asked.

"What?"

"What's your name?" he repeated.

"Tara."

He nodded. "That's better than Millicent, which was your answer the other two times I asked. Here's the deal. I'm gonna cut this duct tape and let you use the john, but if you try to run, next time you can just pee your pants and lay in it."

"I won't run. I can't," Tara whispered. "Please. I need to go."

He eyed her closely as pulled out the switchblade. In two swipes, her hands and feet were free, but when she rolled over to the side of the bed and tried to stand up, she staggered.

He caught her before she hit the floor, then yanked her upright.

"Stand up, damn it."

The derision in his voice was the last straw to what was left of her composure. She grabbed hold of his arm to steady her stance and then looked straight into his eyes with an angry gaze.

"Don't yell at me because I'm unsteady. You're the one who Tased *me*. You're the one who was driving the truck when I was knocked unconscious, and it was you who knocked down the filth in this house that nearly smothered me. You want me steady on my feet? Stay away from me!"

Marshall wanted to be pissed. He didn't like people arguing with him or telling him what to do, but he had to admire her courage.

"You're a tough one, aren't you? Not even cryin' for your mama."

The room was starting to tilt. "My mama is dead. My father is dead. Where's the bathroom?"

He felt guilty for asking and pointed.

"It's behind that door, and don't get any funny ideas about running because I'll be listening. If I don't hear you pee, I'm coming in. Understand?"

Still swaying on her feet, she doubled up her fists.

"If you come in, and my jeans are still down around my ankles, I will fight you until one of us is dead. If it's me, then you won't find your damn money, and I'll be dead and you won't matter. Understand?"

His jaw dropped, and while he was trying to figure out a

comeback for that threat, she staggered into the bathroom and slammed the door shut. He heard the lock turn, but it didn't matter. The window was painted shut, and he'd hear it if she began breaking glass.

He didn't walk close enough to actually hear her pee, but he did hear the toilet flush and then water running in the sink. When she opened the door, she staggered out, carrying a paper cup filled with water.

"My head hurts really bad. Do you have anything for pain?"

"I got some speed."

She groaned. "I have a concussion, not a death wish. Never mind. I'd rather hurt."

He frowned. "I'll see if I can find something in Mom's stuff," he said, and began going through the drawers in the room still full of May Schulter's belongings.

She realized this was the second time he'd referred to his mother. She needed to focus in case she became able to send messages to Flynn.

"Your mother is here?"

"She's in prison. This is her house. Shut up."

Tara sat down on the side of the bed with the cup of water, her fingers trembling as she propped it on her knees for stability.

When Marsh suddenly yelled, she winced, slopping part of the water from the cup onto her pants.

"Hey! Vince! Dig! Get in here!"

Both men came running.

"What's up?" Vince asked.

"Either one of you got anything for pain? I'm not talking about illegal crap. I'm talking aspirin or something like it."

"There's some of that generic kind in the kitchen cabinet," Dig said.

"Go get it," Marsh said, and then glanced over his shoulder at Tara. Except for the tremble in her hands, she was motionless, but he could tell by the way she squinted against the light that she was in pain.

"Here you go," Dig said, as he handed over a nearly full bottle of generic pain meds.

Marsh opened the lid and then handed it to Tara.

"Here, take what you think is safe and then you only got yourself to blame for what happens after."

Tara shook a couple out into her hand, popped them in her mouth, and drank the water.

"Thank you," she whispered, and then lay back down on the bed with her arms covering her head and rolled over onto her side.

"Want something to eat?" Vince asked.

"No. Turn out the light. It makes my head hurt worse."

They looked at each other, then he flipped the switch and walked out of the room.

As soon as they were in the other room, both men started in on Marsh.

"She needs a doctor. She's got a concussion for sure."

Marsh started to slap Vince on the side of the head, then remembered when he'd done it before, Vince said he would leave. Instead, he doubled up his fists and thumped them angrily against his own thighs.

"Well, since we kidnapped her, we can hardly turn around and drive into Stillwater and take her to the doctor now, can we?"

Dig frowned. "Then let's just get her to talk to the ghosts, find out where the money is, and get the hell out of the States while we still can."

Vince glared at Dig. "How do you expect her to commune with the dead when she can't even stay awake?"

"Shut up, the both of you," Marsh said. "All she needs is a good night's sleep. Tomorrow is another day. Now let's all get some rest, okay? And stop freaking out. It's getting on my nerves."

Tara could hear them talking in the other room. Even if she had the luck to find her way out of all the debris, she was too weak to run. Her only hope was that someone found her before it was too late.

She took a deep breath and tried to let go of the pain, but it hurt all the way to her back teeth. Tears rolled from beneath her eyelids and down onto the pillow. As they did, she felt the bed give and then a slight weight against her back, just like when she was little.

"Millicent, is that you?"

She felt a brush of air against her cheek and choked on a sob as she whispered into the darkness. "I can't hear you, and I can't see Henry."

She felt a pat on her arm.

"Will I get better?"

She felt another pat and a hug.

"I'm taking that as a yes."

One more pat and hug.

"Thank God," she muttered, and once again, fell asleep.

IT WAS TWO fifteen in the morning when Detective Allen jumped up from his desk.

"I think I found something!"

Flynn had fallen asleep on an old sofa and got up to see what was happening.

"What is it?" Rutherford asked.

"I pulled May Schulter's phone records for the last six months before she was arrested. There's one number she called every Saturday night as regular as clockwork."

"Who does it belong to?" Rutherford asked.

"It's a number out of Canada."

Rutherford frowned. "So call it."

Flynn grabbed Allen's arm before he could make the call.

"Let me listen to the conversation. I'll hear everything the other person is thinking, even if they don't say it."

Rutherford slapped his hands together.

"This just gets better. Let him listen in," he said.

Allen connected an extension, put his finger to his lips to caution Flynn not to speak, then made the call and put it on speaker.

The phone rang several times. Just when he thought it was going to go to voicemail, he heard a woman answer in a sleepy voice.

"Hello? Hello? Marshall, is that you?"

Allen gave a thumbs-up to the fact that the name matched the one Flynn had overheard.

"No, ma'am. This is the Stillwater Police, in Stillwater, Oklahoma. We're trying to locate Marshall. Is he related to you?"

"Oklahoma? Is that in the States?"

"Yes, ma'am."

"Lord, Lord, I didn't know where he got off to. Is he okay? Has anything happened to him? He's my son."

Flynn grabbed a pen and wrote the word *adopted* on paper.

Rutherford patted him on the back and mouthed, "Good job," while Allen kept on talking.

"I'm sorry. I didn't get your name," Allen said.

"My name is Velma Story."

"Okay, Mrs. Story. When was the last time you talked to Marshall?"

"About two weeks ago. He said he had a business trip out of town. I thought he would call home and at least check on me, but when I didn't hear from him, I began to worry something had happened. Why do you want to talk to him? Is he all right? Has he done something bad?"

"Right now, he's just a name that came up we need to check out. Mrs. Story, I have one more thing to ask. Does the name May Schulter mean anything to you?"

There was a gasp on the other end of the line, and Flynn was frantically writing.

Birth mother.

When Rutherford saw the words, he realized the connection.

"No. I've never heard the name," she said.

Rutherford waved at Allen, signaling him to end the call.

Allen nodded. "I see, well, thank you for your help, and if your son happens to check in, would you please let us know?"

"Yes. Wait a minute while I get a pen and paper," she said.

Flynn covered the phone with his hand. "She's going to try

and call him. If he answers, she's going to warn him that you're looking for him."

Rutherford's smile slipped. "Well damn it, excuse my French, this is not a good development."

As soon as Allen got off the phone, Flynn began filling in the blanks. "The minute you said May Schulter's name, I picked up on fear, anger, and jealousy. She didn't like it that Marshall went looking for his birth mother a few years back, or that they had re-connected. She thinks May is trouble. She doesn't know she's in prison and now assumes he's staying with her, but she's still going to try and warn Marsh you called."

Rutherford was pacing. "Okay, so here's my take on this. During one of their weekly phone calls, May tells Marshall all about this buried money, and then he finds out she's in prison and the money was never recovered. He does a little research and might have found out that Tara was involved in their capture and arrest. If he checked further and found out about the coverage she got during the tornado, he would naturally assume she could lead him straight to the buried cash."

Detective Allen picked up the story. "So he comes here to scope out the situation. The old lady said he'd been gone two weeks, so he's been around here a while. He's located Tara Luna and marked her routine. They're not staying in any of the local motels in the area or rented any trailer houses out at the trailer parks, or their vehicle would have already popped when we put out a BOLO on Tara."

"What about May Schulter's house? I remember my dad talking about her and Nettles all the time before he and Mom got divorced. I think she lives around here," Flynn said.

Rutherford stopped pacing and looked at Flynn. "You *are* freakin' cop material, I tell you. If you don't go into law enforcement, you're gonna be missing your calling. Allen, find out if May Schulter owned any property in the area. I'm contacting Captain Farrell to let him know what's happening."

He slapped Flynn on the back and then pointed at his desk. "Help yourself to doughnuts and coffee in the lounge."

"Uh, there's one other thing," Flynn said.

Both men stopped.

"Like what?" Rutherford said.

"I know this sounds weird, but you guys are used to Tara's abilities, right?"

They shrugged and nodded.

"So, my dad's spirit has been trying to contact me to tell me where the missing money is. Tara said his energy is low which is why he kept fading in and out and not making much sense, but he told us that my mom knows where he hid the money."

They were dumbstruck.

"You mean she's been in on this from the first?" Rutherford asked.

"No, only that she would know where he'd hidden it when he gave Tara the clues."

"What were the clues?" Allen asked.

"He said he hid it, and it's with Aunt Tillie."

"What did Mona say when you told her that?"

"She said she knew what that meant. So, I guess when you guys are ready to recover it, just ask her."

"Just like that? Just ask her?" Rutherford muttered.

Allen glanced at his partner. "I need to give the DEA a heads up. They're the ones who will coordinate the retrieval."

Flynn sighed. "Mom is already so mad at Dad for involving us in his criminal activities. This is going to send her over the edge."

"Yeah, well, I still need to go talk to the captain. Hang around, kid. You're turning out to be as handy as a pocket on a shirt," Rutherford said, and left to call the captain.

Allen was on the phone with the DEA.

Flynn headed for the break room. Coffee and doughnuts sounded good, and then the minute he thought it, Tara's face slid through his mind, and just like that, his appetite was gone. Was she hungry? Was she cold? Were they hurting her?

Come on, sweetheart. Come on, Tara. Talk to me. Please talk to me.

THE TRIO HAD cleared a few areas in the house for easier

access when they first arrived, but with their kidnap victim in Marsh's bed, there was no place left to sleep.

Marsh had fallen asleep in an easy chair in front of the television. Dig was sacked out in a sleeping bag nearby, and Vince was asleep in the other chair.

When Marsh's phone began to ring, he jumped like he'd been shot. No one here knew his number, and with both of his buddies in the same room, it wouldn't be them trying to call. That left his mother, and he didn't want to talk. When it finally quit ringing, he glanced down and realized she'd left a message.

"Damn," he muttered, and went into his voicemail to hear the message. The moment he heard her voice, he knew she was beyond mad, and then the longer he listened, the more panicked he became.

MARSHALL, IT'S YOUR mother. I realize you are a grown man and don't answer to me, but I wanted you to know that I am well aware you are in Oklahoma with May Schulter. I don't see your fascination with someone who just gave you away like that. I should let you stew in whatever mess you are concocting, but I can't. You are my son. I love you. I wish you could at least give me the respect I deserve. However, the real reason I called is to let you know that the Stillwater Police just called me, wanting to know where you were. What have you been doing? Call me.

Marsh came up out of the chair as if he'd been catapulted.

"Wake up! Wake up!" he yelled, and kicked Dig in the backside, then turned around and shook Vince's shoulder. "Wake up! We've got trouble!"

Both men began scrambling.

"What? What's happening?" Vince said.

"The Stillwater cops are on to us! That little psychic bitch must be playing us for dummies and somehow sending messages to the cops about who snatched her."

"How do you know?" Dig asked.

"That phone call was from Mama, back in Canada. The cops called her, asking for me. I don't know what she told them, but she called to warn me they were looking for me. We've got to get out of here."

"But it's dark, and it's too cold to hide out in the woods somewhere. Where would we go?" Vince asked. "If they know your name, they will know what you're driving. You've got a Canadian tag on the truck, and the only other thing on the property with wheels is the old tractor."

"Don't argue. Just start packing! I'm going to talk to that bitch. I'll make her sorry for playing us like this."

"Don't hurt her any more. You'll wind up killing her, and I didn't sign up for any murder," Vince shouted.

Marsh stomped out of the room without answering, stormed into the room where Tara was sleeping, and turned on the lights.

"Wake the hell up!" he yelled. "We need to talk!"

Tara moaned, covering her eyes as she rolled over and slowly accustomed herself to the unexpected brightness. "Please don't yell," she whispered.

He grabbed her by the arm. "There's nothing wrong with you. You've been playing us for losers. I want to know how you do it."

Tara's head was spinning as she tried to sit up. "Do what? I don't know what you're talking about."

"How do the Stillwater cops know our names? Who have you contacted? We never searched you. Where's your phone?"

He yanked her to her feet and began feeling her up, running his hands all over her body trying to find a cell phone.

She made a fist and punched him in the nose. Blood spurted from his nose as she fell backward from the impact, holding her fist from the pain.

"You broke my nose!" he screamed.

"You keep your hands off of me!" she screamed back. "I told you I'd fight until one of us is dead. Did you think I didn't mean it?"

He doubled up his fist, but before he could swing, the window near the bed suddenly shattered, and a huge shard of glass came flying through the air and into his shoulder.

He screamed again and ran out of the room.

Tara covered her face and started sobbing. "Millicent! Henry! You saved me! You saved me!"

She felt a soft breeze circling her and then an intense energy flow through her body. They were trying to give her strength.

She got to her feet and began looking for her coat. If she found a way out, she was taking it. She'd rather die from exposure than spend one more second under the roof with these creeps.

She walked out of the bedroom, stumbling through the tiny aisles between the hoarder-stacked bags and boxes stacked ceiling high along the walls and followed the sounds of voices into the kitchen. The three men were at the sink with their backs to her, occupied with pulling the glass shard from Marsh's shoulder and putting on a pressure bandage to stifle the blood flow.

She saw her coat on top of some boxes near the back door and made her move. She had it in her hand and was running when Marsh saw her.

"Hey! Stop her!"

Both Vince and Dig leaped forward and caught her before she reached the door. They dragged her back to the table and shoved her down in a chair while Marsh glanced nervously around the room, afraid more windows would be shattering.

Tara felt defeated. *Flynn! I need help. Can you hear me? They're going to run.*

"Did you make that glass fly?" he asked.

Flynn didn't answer, or if he did, she couldn't hear. She lifted her chin, unwilling to let them know how scared she was.

"No. That's telekinesis, and I can't make things move. My ghosts did that. They don't take kindly to people hurting me."

"So how have you been contacting the police?"

Tara rolled her eyes. "That's sending mental messages to other people, and I can't do that either. I just see and talk to ghosts."

"Then how do the cops know my name?"

"How should I know?"

Tara folded her arms and laid her head down on the table.

She wanted to think that Flynn was picking up on her thoughts and she just couldn't hear him, but there was also the possibility that wasn't happening, because she hadn't been able to focus like that.

Then her eyes fell on his cell phone, and it hit her. "My phone."

He turned around. "What about your phone? Where is it?"

"I was talking on the phone when you two kidnapped me, remember?"

Marsh thought back and then groaned.

"I dropped it in the snow when you Tased me. But the person I was talking to had to hear me scream, and he most likely heard everything you two said while you were dragging me to your truck. If you called each other by a name, he would have heard that, too. If the cops know names, you gave yourselves away. I didn't do it."

Vince and Marsh stared at each other, trying to remember what they'd said, but guessed she was right.

"So now what?" Vince asked.

"We run," Marsh said, and pointed at Tara. "And we're taking her with us."

Tara stood up, nearly as tall as Marsh, and pointed back.

"If you hurt me again, the next time that glass will be in your throat."

Marsh was trapped—too scared to ignore her threat, and at the same time, in too big a mess to chance leaving her behind and make a run for the border.

"Shut up," he muttered. "Just shut up."

Tara glared. "Then leave me alone."

He turned his back on her.

Too weak to stand up any longer, she sat back down with a thump and listened to them planning to go to a new location—a place they'd found days earlier while sightseeing in the area. She heard enough to know what direction they planned to take and waited until they were about ready to walk out the door before she dared chance leaving behind a clue for the police.

"Is it okay if I use the bathroom one more time before we

go?"

"Get it over with," Marsh said, and even followed her into the bedroom to make sure she didn't try to get out the broken window.

She locked the bathroom door and used the bathroom, well aware it might be hours before they'd stop to let her go again, and while the toilet was flushing, she found a tube of lip gloss in the medicine cabinet and wrote the highway and direction on the mirror and quickly came out, closing the door behind her. Afraid he might be inclined to go next, she walked swiftly pass Marsh, giving him the impression that she was thinking about making a run for it in the dark once they got outside, and it worked.

He grabbed her by the arm and escorted her out of the house and into the backseat of the pickup truck. The other two had been unloading the firewood to make room for the bags they tossed in the truck bed. They got in, putting Dig in the backseat with Tara. Because of Marsh's wound, Vince was in the driver's seat. It was after 4:00 a.m. when they finally drove away.

Chapter Seven

DETECTIVE ALLEN made the call to the DEA and gave them the info on Mona O'Mara and then began searching property records on May Schulter.

Flynn eyed the tall, dark-haired detective staring intently at his computer screen and decided this was a good time to give his mother a heads-up on what was happening. When he made the call, she answered so quickly he knew she must have been sleeping with her phone right by her hand.

"Hello?"

"Mom, it's me."

Mona threw back her cover and sat up, running her fingers through the flat side of her hair as she recognized her son's voice. "Do you know anything?"

"Some stuff. We know who took her and why, but we don't know where they are."

"Oh, my lord," Mona said. "Pat is beside himself, and there's nothing that will make this better until Tara comes home."

"Are you still there?"

"Yes. I bunked down on the sofa after Pat finally went to his room."

"I need you to know that I told the police about Dad's message and that you understood the clues."

She groaned.

"I'm sorry, Mom."

"No. It has to be done, and we want this over with once and for all."

"The police notified the DEA. It's their case, so one of their agents will be contacting you."

"Okay. Thank you for letting me know."

Flynn looked up and saw Rutherford coming back into the room.

"Yeah . . . hey, Mom. I gotta go. I'll call again if I know something."

Rutherford waved Flynn over and then headed for Allen's desk.

"Find anything?" Rutherford asked.

He nodded. "There's a homestead exemption filed in her name. I have a legal description of the property, and I'm running a search to find out exactly where it is on the county map."

"This is good! Right?"

"It's progress," Allen said.

Flynn was watching the computer screen when all of a sudden he heard Tara's voice.

Flynn! Can you hear me? They're going to run.

Tara! Tara! Yes! Can you hear me?

When she didn't answer, he groaned, but one thing was good. He'd heard her again. Whatever was wrong with her might be clearing up.

"What's up, kid?" Rutherford asked.

"I just heard her voice. I answered, but she didn't respond like she usually does."

They both turned and looked at him.

"Are you serious?" Rutherford asked.

Flynn frowned. "About what?"

"You two are tuned into each other's thoughts all the time?"

"If we want to," he said.

"Holy Moses," Allen said softly. "What if you're thinking stuff you don't want her to hear?"

He shrugged. "I still can't control it, so she hears it. The saving grace is not following through on the thought."

"Gotcha," Allen said, still shaking his head, and then he jumped as his computer search ended. "Hey! I got a hit on that legal description."

"Is it close?" Flynn asked.

"About six miles west of Stillwater then back south."

"Let's go! She said they were going to run! We have to hurry!" Flynn yelled.

"Wait, wait, kid. We're not going in cold. We need backup to make sure we don't make matters worse for her, if they're even still there. If Marsh Story's mother called him after we talked to her, they have almost a two hour warning. We have to call county. That's the sheriff's domain."

A sudden blur of tears clouded Flynn's vision. "They have to still be there," he said, and then shoved his hands in his pockets and turned away.

IT WAS NEARING 5:00 a.m. when three cars from the county sheriff's department pulled into the driveway of the house. Detectives Rutherford and Allen, with Flynn in the back seat pulled up behind them.

Lights were shining from the front windows, but there were no vehicles in sight. A large pile of firewood had been dumped at the corner of the yard near an old tractor, and there was a set of tire tracks leading out. They were still uncertain if this had been the place where Marshall Story and his sidekicks had been hanging out, but they would soon find out.

Deputies quietly fanned out around the house as two of them approached the front door, then knocked sharply.

"Payne County Sheriff's Department! Open the door!"

Flynn was holding his breath, praying she would still be there under guard. But no one answered.

The deputies repeated the demand, and as they knocked, the door swung inward.

"It's not locked!" they yelled, and moved inward with guns drawn, shouting their presence as they went. Moments later they came back out. "It's empty!" they yelled.

"Damn it," Rutherford said.

"I'm going inside," Flynn said.

"Look, kid, this is police business and—"

"You wouldn't even be here without me," Flynn said, and shoved passed them and strode toward the house.

The detectives took off after him, and when one of the deputies started to block him from entering, Rutherford held up his badge.

"Let him pass."

The trio stopped only a few feet inside the doorway, stunned by the hoarder aspect of the interior.

"Have mercy!" Allen said.

Rutherford frowned as a rat slipped out from behind a pile of garbage bags and made a run toward a stack of boxes.

"Rats! Oh damn, I hate rats!" he muttered.

Flynn kept thinking of Tara being held captive in a place like this and started winding his way through the narrow passageways. When he got to the kitchen and saw blood all over the floor, the cabinet, and the sink, his legs nearly went out from under him.

A deputy pointed to a large shard of glass on the counter. "This is bloody, and there's a broken window in the other room. Someone got cut, maybe trying to escape."

Flynn swallowed past the knot in his throat and kept thinking Tara's name, praying she would answer, but she didn't. When he walked into the bedroom, Rutherford made a beeline for the broken window. It didn't take him long to assess the scene.

"This didn't break from someone trying to get out. All the glass is inside on the floor, which means it shattered inward, not out."

Flynn saw blood on the bed and then gritted his teeth and looked away. He flashed on the day they'd found Bethany Fanning out in that cabin by the lake where she'd been kidnapped. She had endured hell on earth, lived through it, and was thriving today. Whatever they did to Tara couldn't matter, as long as she was alive.

He turned away, and as he did, saw something glitter on the wall. He moved closer and started to rub a finger across the wall and then pulled it back in sudden shock, startled by the pain and the sudden spurt of blood. "What the heck?" he yelled.

"What's wrong, kid?" Allen asked.

Flynn pointed at the walls. "Look at the walls on this side of the room. They are embedded with bits of glass."

Rutherford tentatively touched the wall with the same reaction as Flynn.

"What in the hell, excuse my French, could do this?"

Flynn thought about the huge shard of glass in the kitchen and the glass in the walls, and then it hit him.

Tara's ghosts! He glanced around to make sure he wasn't overheard then lowered his voice.

"I know how this happened. It was her ghosts. You know what they do when someone is dissing her, or trying to harm her. There's a little blood on the bed, but not much. But there's a whole lot of blood that starts here at the door and goes all the way into the kitchen."

Rutherford took in the situation, still uneasy about believing in the ghosts and wanting to find another reason. But the kid was right. The blood on the bed wasn't much. Like what you'd get from a busted lip or a nose bleed. The big blood trail began just inside the door and then went all the way into the kitchen to the sink.

"Do you really think ghosts could make this happen?" Rutherford asked.

Allen punched him on the arm.

"Seriously? You're still asking? We've been victims ourselves of flying paper. Remember those times in the principal's office at her school and inside her house? If they can make paper fly and open and slam doors, they can do the same to windows."

Rutherford still didn't comment.

The bathroom door was ajar, obviously when they'd searched the house for occupants, but it was dark inside. All of a sudden, a light popped on inside it.

"Who's in there?" Flynn asked.

A deputy was going through papers on a dresser and turned as Flynn pointed.

"No one's in there," he said.

"Someone is. A light just came on," Flynn said.

Both detectives and the deputy pulled their guns and started toward the bathroom. When the deputy shoved the door aside and stepped in, he paused and yelled back.

"It's empty."

Flynn shook his head. He hadn't been tuned into the spirit world long, but he knew they could manipulate energy, and electricity was energy personified. It had to be Tara's ghosts. Maybe there was something in there they wanted him to see.

The deputy exited as Flynn walked in. The tub was missing a shower curtain, and the tiny shelf where towels might have been stored was missing doors. There was no place to hide.

He looked back toward the sink, then all around the floor. Other than dirt and trash, he saw nothing obvious. The door to the medicine cabinet was shut, and when he reached to open it, he grimaced at the grease all over the edge. He pulled back his hands to wipe it off and as he did, caught the scent of strawberry.

"What the heck?" he said, as he smelled of his fingers. The greasy stuff was scented. So, what was greasy and scented? Then it hit him. Lip gloss! He'd kissed it off Tara's lips often enough to know.

He glanced up at the mirror. It was just as greasy. He opened the door with two fingers, and as the mirrored door moved into a different perspective, he thought he saw a word written on the glass.

"Hey! Hey, guys!"

The cops came running.

He pointed.

"I think there's something written on the mirror in lip gloss. Maybe Tara left us message."

Rutherford looked. "Son of a gun! I see words, but I can't make them out."

"Hang on," Allen said and ran out of the room.

They heard doors banging in the kitchen, and then a few moments later he was back with a jar of instant coffee granules.

"Stand back," he said.

Flynn stepped into the tub as the deputy and Rutherford moved back to the doorway.

Allen flung the contents of the jar toward the mirror in a sweeping motion, covering the sink and floor in ground-roasted coffee powder, but it had also stuck to every greasy streak on the mirror.

"Freakin' brilliant!" Rutherford said, and took a picture with his cell phone.

Flynn read it out loud. "Hiway 51 East. Keystone."

"That's got to be Keystone Lake," Rutherford said. "I guess she's telling us that's where they're headed."

"I'll tell the sheriff. He can alert OHP," the deputy said.

And just like that, the Oklahoma Highway Patrol was now involved in the investigation.

Flynn glanced up at the mirror as they filed out of the tiny bathroom, imagining the fear Tara must have been feeling as she wrote that on the mirror, not knowing if they would find it, or if it would even matter in case they didn't find her in time. But it had given him new insight into the girl with whom he'd fallen in love. No matter what was thrown at her, she kept fighting. He could do no less.

Way to go, Moon Girl.

Flynn? Flynn, is that you?

THE EXTENDED CAB of the pickup truck was handy, but obviously not built for long-legged people. Tara's knees were pressed hard against the back of the driver's seat, and her head was still throbbing. Even worse, there was less than a foot of space between her and Dig, and he needed a bath.

The whole time they were driving toward the highway, she had been praying they'd meet a parade of cop cars coming to her rescue, but to her dismay they did not meet another vehicle until they reached Highway 51. They were going to have to go through Stillwater to get to Keystone. If God was paying attention to her plight, maybe they'd be stopped on their way through town, but that didn't happen either. When they passed the city limits sign on the east side of town and disappeared into the night, Tara turned her face to the window, unwilling for them to see her cry.

The miles sped by with only flashes of light to mark their passing, sometimes from security lights on front porches, and other times by the lights of an oncoming car. The snowy highway had been slushy during the day, but refrozen, they were now driving on ice.

Tara was so tired that both her body and mind were on standby. If she didn't hurt so bad, she would have been hungry. She hadn't eaten since the pancakes the morning before and turned slightly sideways in the seat, no longer opposed to touching Dig's legs in an effort to ease the misery of her situation. Her back was to the window and her eyes were closed. She was using the top of the seat for a pillow and could hear the men talking among themselves about what they would do with that missing money when it was found, when all of a sudden, she heard Flynn's voice as clear as day.

Way to go, Moon Girl.

Her eyes popped open.

OMG! *Flynn? Flynn, is that you?*

Yes, baby, yes, it's me. Where are you?

Driving East toward Keystone Lake.

We just found your message.

She stifled a sob. If only they'd come sooner.

We saw the blood. Are you okay?

It belongs to Marsh. He hit me, made my nose and lip bleed, and Millicent flipped out on him.

Why couldn't I hear you before? What's wrong?

Tara was so elated to be hearing him that it was all she could do to stay still.

I think I have a concussion. I can't hear Millicent or see Henry. I've never been this alone in my entire life. I couldn't hear you until just now.

I hear you, too, thank God. Every time you see a new landmark, let me know. I don't know how far ahead of us you are, but we will find you.

Maybe not in time. In my dream, I died.

Don't give up on me, Tara, and I won't give up on you.

I love you, Flynn. Tell Uncle Pat I love him, too.

I love you, too, and you can tell him yourself. Every time you see a landmark, just say what you see. I'll tell the others.

Yes. Okay.

Silence.

It felt as if the weight of the world had just shifted off her shoulders. She was no longer in this alone. "Thank God," she said softly.

"What did you say?" Dig asked.

"I wasn't talking to you," Tara said.

Marsh smirked. "I heard her. She was praying to God, but she needs to be praying that it's O'Mara's ghost who answers her call."

The men laughed among themselves.

Tara clenched her jaw and then kicked at Dig's leg to make a little more room for her own.

"Hey," he yelped.

She just pulled her coat up around her ears and kept her eyes on the road in front of them. Reconnecting with Flynn gave her hope that there might be a better end to this mess after all.

Chapter Eight

THE MOMENT FLYNN lost the connection with Tara, he headed for the cops. There was no way he could keep what he did a secret anymore and still help her, but what he wanted was no longer an issue.

"I just heard from Tara! She said—"

The sheriff grabbed him by the arm. "She called you? Why didn't you let us talk to her?"

"It's not like that," Flynn said. "I didn't—"

Rutherford waved the sheriff off. "Just tell us what she said, kid. We'll explain the rest to the sheriff."

The sheriff glared at the two detectives. He didn't like being overruled, especially by city cops.

Flynn began repeating what she'd said.

"They're on Highway 51 going east toward Keystone Lake. Most of the blood belongs to Marshall Story. Tara said when he hit her, Millicent went ballistic on him. Tara has a concussion, which is why I haven't been able to communicate. And, she says she can't hear Millicent or see Henry, and she's pretty freaked out about that."

Rutherford sighed. "This is good news. Thank God that girl is okay."

The sheriff had had enough.

"Okay, start explaining about a call that isn't a call, and who the hell are Millicent and Henry?"

Rutherford sighed. "They're her ghosts."

The sheriff laughed, and then when he realized he was the only one laughing, he choked. "Are you freakin' serious? You want me to believe she has ghosts? And what does her concussion have to do with not being able to talk, and didn't you guys find her phone at the site of the abduction, so whose phone is she using?"

Rutherford shrugged. "Don't much care what you believe. I'm just answering your question. She couldn't talk to the kid here because they communicate by thought, and she doesn't need a phone to think. Don't ask for further explanations because believe me, they only get more complicated. I don't know what you county guys are going to do, but I have my captain's permission to chase this down. Detective Allen and I are taking the kid here, and we're going to follow that girl until we find her. She never quit on us when we needed her help, and we're damn sure not going to quit on her."

Flynn heard all he needed to hear and made a run for their vehicle. He was already in the back seat and buckled up when the detectives reached the car. Allen got something out of the trunk as Rutherford got in behind the wheel.

"Are you up for this, kid?" Rutherford asked.

"Yes."

"Is your Mama gonna whip our butts for taking you with us?"

"No, but I will let her know."

Allen got in with a small ice chest. He handed a can of pop to Flynn, one to Rutherford, and kept one for himself.

"It's caffeine, kid. Drink up. It's after 5:00 in the morning, and we haven't slept in over twenty-four hours. You're gonna need it."

Flynn did as he was told, sipping the cold pop as they took off out of the yard, slinging snow and slush as they sped away.

"There are candy bars in the console," Rutherford said.

Allen passed one around to each of them.

Flynn called his mom as they drove, giving her an update on everything that had happened, where they were going, and that he loved her.

Mona was trying not to be hysterical, but he'd been in ICU less than three months ago on the verge of death. This seemed too drastic, too soon.

"You're not doing anything that will get you hurt again, are you?"

"Mom, I'm in the back of a cop car helping them find Tara. You know I have to be a part of this."

"I don't understand how they expect you to find her any better than they can. I think—"

"It's complicated, Mom, and I'll explain it to you after this is over. Just trust me when I say I may be the only way we'll get her back. I love you. Talk to you later."

"I love you, too," Mona said, and when the line went dead, she disconnected with a frown.

Pat was sitting at the kitchen table beside her, nursing a cup of coffee. He'd been watching her expressions all the way through the conversation, trying to read the mood and hoping it was good news about Tara.

"Was that Flynn? What did he say? Did they find her?"

"They found the place where they'd been holding her, but they're gone. Tara left them a message on a bathroom mirror. They're in pursuit."

Pat lowered his head, his voice shaking. "I have never wanted a drink as bad in my life as I do right now."

Mona leaned over and put her arms around his neck and just held him. "You are the strongest, kindest man I've ever known, and you will continue to be strong because Tara needs you. I need you."

Pat shuddered, then turned around and wrapped his arms around her. "I need you, too," he said.

A few moments later, there was a knock at the door.

Pat jumped up to answer, hoping it would be the police with better news. Instead, it was Nate Pierce.

"Is it true?" Nate asked.

Pat nodded. "How did you find out?"

"I guess it's all over town. Her friend Nikki called me. I don't know how she found out." Nate groaned and shoved a hand through his hair in disbelief. "I just saw her at the university yesterday afternoon. I offered to give her a ride home, and she said she wanted to walk. It was cold. I should have insisted."

"It's no more your fault than it is mine for the fact that I watched her go out the front door, expecting she would come back. Come inside. I have coffee."

Nate shook his head. "No. I have to go tell the others. They are waiting for word to begin the drumming. We will be praying for her safe return."

Breath caught in the back of Pat's throat. "Thank you."

Nate shook his head. "No, my family and people thank her. She is one of the chosen ones. The Old Ones will hear our drums. They'll hear our prayers and guide Tara to safety."

Pat's eyes filled with tears.

Nate handed him a card. "This has my number. Call me when she's home."

Pat watched him make a run for his car and drive off. When he went back to the kitchen, Mona was frying bacon.

"Who was that?" she asked.

"That geology professor from the college. You remember him, right?"

"Nate Pierce? Yes, I remember him."

Pat got out a loaf of bread for the toaster. "He's a great guy, but he obviously lives with one foot in the white man's world and the other in his native culture. He said he was going back to tell the others to start the drumming, and something about Old Ones."

Mona paused. "Then he's doubly blessed. Not all of us are as connected to our ancestors as is the Native American."

"Tara is. She has a hot line to all of them, whether she likes it or not."

Just her name on his lips choked him up. He turned away, unable to say more.

AS SOON AS Rutherford left the snow-covered road to turn onto Highway 51, he hit the lights and siren and stomped the gas.

Pop slopped out of the can onto the legs of Flynn's jeans, but he didn't care. He was focused on Tara, listening for the sound of her voice.

TARA GLANCED AT the clock on the dashboard of the truck. It was nearly six. It wouldn't be long before sunrise. She hoped it got light before they found a place to stop. She'd have a better chance of giving him directions.

Marsh was dozing up front, high on speed he'd taken in an effort to dull the pain of the wound in his shoulder. Dig was snoring in the seat beside Tara, leaving her and Vince the only two awake. She caught the man looking at her more than once in the rearview mirror, but couldn't tell by his expression if he was of a mind to cut her throat or let her go. When she caught him staring, she stared back until he was the one forced to look away.

Her gaze shifted to the faint glow of headlights on the dark highway. She shuddered and made herself focus on anything but the choking fear of her situation.

Within seconds, she heard Vince curse and caught a glimpse of flashing lights in the rearview mirror a distance behind them. Her heart leaped. The OHP had found them. Thank God.

"Marsh! Wake up!" Vince yelled, and gave him a sharp jab on the shoulder. "It's the cops! They're coming up behind us."

Marsh woke up with a curse and a groan as Dig turned to look.

"Maybe he's just running hot toward a wreck or something. Maybe he's not coming after us," Dig said.

Tara didn't want that to be the case.

Flynn! We're still on Highway 51, and there's a highway patrol car a good distance behind us. Did he make us, or is he on his way to somewhere else?

Don't know. I'll check.

"Are you willing to take that chance?" Vince yelled. "Say the word, Marsh! What do we do?"

Marsh was just drugged up enough to be dangerous. "Turn off the lights! Now!"

Tara gasped. *OMG, no!*

Vince freaked. "Are you crazy?"

"Turn off the damn lights!" Marsh screamed.

Vince hit the switch, and all of a sudden they were in darkness, flying into the night without a guide.

Dig lowered his head, closed his eyes, and started praying for mercy.

"Stop! Stop! You're going to kill us," Tara shouted.

What's happening? What's happening?

Overwhelmed by panic, Tara couldn't focus enough to answer Flynn.

Marsh was on his knees, looking out the back. The patrol car was still coming.

"Faster!" Marsh shouted. "We have to stay far enough ahead of the cop's headlights, or he'll see us anyway."

Vince stomped the accelerator.

It was like being launched into the darkness of outer space. All of a sudden there was no sense of speed or place, just the whistle of air and the thump and whine of tires on the icy pavement.

When they went airborne, Tara screamed.

Marsh was braced for a crash, and Dig was crying loudly.

Vince had a death grip on the steering wheel, as if he could control what was happening by the strength of his grip alone.

When the impact came, it was not what any of them expected. They cleared a bar ditch with a bone-jarring thump and drove straight through a barbed wire fence into a snow-covered pasture.

"No brakes, no brakes! They'll see the lights," Marsh screamed.

Vince's jaw was set as he did a 180 to the right, turning the truck completely around until they were facing the highway with a front-row seat to the patrol car still a quarter of a mile behind.

Tara was so elated to still be breathing that she didn't even care when the cop flew past without stopping, but Marsh and Vince were shouting with glee, giving each other a high-five that they'd escaped arrest.

"I think I peed my pants," Vince muttered.

"Turn the lights back on, and let's get the hell out of here,"

Marsh said.

Tara! Tara! What the hell is happening?

We ran off the road into a pasture, but the cop lost us. He's gone.

The headlights highlighted their situation, as well as a half-dozen head of cattle thirty yards to their left. They seemed to be staring curiously at what had appeared in their midst.

"Look at that! If we'd driven into that herd, we'd be toast," Vince said.

Dig was still crying.

"Dig! Shut the hell up. We're fine," Marsh said.

"We're not fine," Dig shouted. "We're criminals on the run, and you're going to get us killed."

Marsh's voice lowered menacingly. "I said, shut up."

Dig swiped the snot off his lip with the back of his hand, and sat up straighter.

Vince glanced up in the rearview mirror at Tara.

She lifted her chin.

He looked away, put the truck in gear and slipped and slid their way out of the pasture and back onto the highway.

Marsh slapped his leg and then winced when motion hurt his shoulder, but he was bugged by the fact that the girl was so calm.

"So, ghosty girl, what do you have to say about that fine piece of maneuvering?" he asked.

"That the cows are going to get out."

Marsh's smirk ended. "Bitch," he muttered.

It put a damper on the high of their car chase, and the adrenaline crash afterward ended their chatter.

Only after the danger of a wreck was over did Tara let go of her emotions. She was shaking so hard it was difficult to draw breath. Tears were blurring her vision, and her hands were clutched into fists.

Never let them see you cry.

Tara jumped. *Millicent! OMG! I can finally hear you, too!*

You had to let go of the pain. The panic did it.

Is Flynn close to me?

Not close, but coming.

Marshall is going to kill me. I saw it in my sleep.

This isn't over. Stop expecting the worst. Look ahead. Tell Flynn what you see.

Tara looked through the windshield and saw lights. *Flynn, I can see lights. We're coming up on some kind of city, but it can't be Tulsa. Not enough lights.*

Got that. Hang on.

There were a few moments of silence as she waited.

Rutherford said it might be Mannford. We are nearly an hour behind you.

Oh no.

No. It's okay. We're running hot, lights and sirens. We'll make up the time soon.

Tara leaned back in the seat, her eyes burning from lack of sleep and the dull thud of the headache still pounding relentlessly. And just when she was at another low point, Henry popped up in the seat between her and Dig.

She gasped and then smiled. Henry kissed her soundly on the cheek, making the whole side of her face tingle smartly, then promptly punched Dig in the nose.

Dig woke up with a grunt, brushing at his nose in confusion. "What happened?" he muttered.

Tara was staring out the window on her left.

Dig frowned. "Hey. What did you do to me?"

She frowned. "Nothing."

"Somebody poked me in the nose."

"It wasn't me."

Henry winked at Tara and then did it again.

Dig's head bobbed back against the window with a *thunk*. Although it had happened again, this time he'd been looking straight at the girl, and her arms were folded across her chest, her hands tucked beneath them for warmth.

Vince looked up in the rearview mirror. "What's going on back there?"

Dig plastered himself against the other side of seat, as far away from Tara as he could get. "Something is poking me in the face."

Vince looked at Tara. "Are you crazy, girl?"

"It's not me, and he knows it."

Dig's eyes were wide and fixed on Tara. "She didn't do it. I was watching her."

Marsh grunted. "Stop whining. Are you bleeding?"

"No."

"Then shut up."

Henry slapped Vince on the back of the head.

"Hey!" Vince said, and then swerved sharply when he realized he'd almost run off the road.

Tara rolled her eyes. "Henry, stop playing with them, or they'll wreck and kill us all."

"Who's Henry?" Vince asked.

"My other ghost."

Dig went ballistic. "Oh shit, oh no, oh dang it, Vince. Let's go home. I wanna go back to Toronto. This was a crazy plan anyway."

Marsh felt the same way, but they had a problem. She knew what they looked like, and they'd be on the run the rest of their lives if they just let her go and ran. He didn't have the stomach for murder, but he knew it was coming to that. He turned and looked at Tara. "You're getting better, aren't you? I mean, you can do your psychic thing again now?"

"It's coming back, yes," Tara said.

"Good. As soon as we get settled, you contact O'Mara's spirit and find out what he did with that money."

"I can only try. I told you before that he doesn't know me or owe me anything."

"Hey, isn't this our turn?" Vince asked, pointing to a lighted billboard on their left.

Tara looked. It was a turnoff to the lake.

Flynn. Brush Creek. Three miles west of Mannford on 51. North on 151.

I heard you. Stay with me, baby.

Just don't lose me.

Never.

"It's a good thing we went sightseeing last week," Marsh

said, and then moaned. "Damn, my shoulder hurts."

The noose was tightening, and Tara knew it. They obviously had another destination in mind, and once they got stopped, her fate was in question. If and when she got anything out of Michael O'Mara they would consider her a liability and get rid of her.

We're both here. Hang rough.

It's hang tough, Millicent.

Whatever, just hang with us, honey. We've got your butt.

Tara stifled a grin.

That's back . . . you say, we've got your back, not butt.

Tara heard a slight pop. Millicent had tuned out, but knowing they were close gave her courage.

There was a faint glow in the east, a reminder that night was giving way to the inevitable sunrise. She could see just enough of the pristine beauty of untracked snow to think that the heavily wooded area had a fairy tale appearance. If felt weird to be in so much danger in such a beautiful place.

"How far do I go?" Vince asked.

Marsh was swigging down a handful of some kind of pills with what was left of the beer in his can.

Tara hoped it was an overdose that would either knock him out or kill him. She wasn't picky.

"Just keep driving until I tell you different," Marsh mumbled.

"Then stop popping pills, or you'll pass out and I still won't know," Vince snapped.

Marsh glared.

Tara shifted; her long legs were aching from being cooped up so long. When she moved, Dig jumped like he'd been slapped again, and then pulled himself into the far corner of the back seat and put his hand over his face, just in case.

Tara mentally counted off the miles at every section line.

Flynn, we've gone a little more than three miles north so far.

I hear you.

Wait! We're turning, west. Look for a pair of tall pines at the mailbox. It's a narrow one-lane road with fences on both sides.

Got it. Keep talking to me.

Tara kept waiting, but the road went on for almost a mile before an outbuilding appeared. It was the back of an old barn. As they came around the curve she could see the house.

Long road to the house. You'll see an old barn first and then an A-frame log cabin. It looks empty. Oh God.

What?

I have a bad feeling.

No. No. We're close. Keep the faith. We're coming.

"We're here, boys and girls," Vince drawled.

Tara's heart was hammering as they opened the doors. She unfolded her legs, wincing as she swung them down, then out of the truck.

Marsh pointed at her. "Grab her arm. I don't want her trying to run."

"Let me go," Tara muttered, and yanked her arm free. "The only place I want to go is to a bathroom."

Marsh started to argue, but the moment they touched her, a whirlwind came up out of the snow behind him like a genie out of a bottle, and once again, he was being battered, this time by icy pellets.

"Get her inside!" he yelled, and made a run for the cabin.

The first time he'd come here, he'd made a point of finding a way in and leaving the front door unlocked. If it was still unlocked, it was his clue that no one had been here.

It swung inward with ease, and he slammed it shut behind them. The blast of snow hit the front of the cabin as soon as they slammed the door, and then it was over.

Dig was crying all over again, but this time no one was yelling at him. Even Marsh looked rattled. There was no way to fight something that didn't exist in the physical form.

The interior of the A-frame was all one big room with a staircase that led up to a landing on the second floor.

Still rattled from what happened outside, Marsh pointed a finger in Tara's face. "Tell that damn ghost to stop or I'll—"

"You'll what?" Tara asked. "The last time you made me bleed, she nearly cut your throat. You ready for a second round?"

"Damn it!" Marsh yelled, and then slammed his fist into the back of an old leather chair.

"Does anybody know where the bathroom is?" Tara asked.

"Take her down the hall and stand outside the door." He pointed at Tara. "You have one minute."

Worn out and ready for all of this to be over, Tara reacted in disgust. "Are you going to kill me?"

All three men stopped in their tracks.

"Well? Are you? Because if you are, then do it and get it over with. I'm tired and I'm sick and I'm hungry. I haven't eaten in over twenty-four hours. And I need more than a minute inside that bathroom. Figure the rest out for yourself."

She stomped off down the hall without waiting for an escort, opened one door which turned out to be a closet, kept going until she found the bathroom, and slammed the door behind her when she went inside.

"What the hell are we going to do with her?" Dig muttered. "She's not scared of any of us. Her ghosts are playing hell with my nerves and will likely kill us all if you lay a hand on her."

"They can't kill us," Marsh muttered.

A framed picture of an elk flew off the wall and hit Marsh in the back of the head before anyone could warn him what was happening. Once again, glass shattered as he dropped to the floor, moaning.

Dig made a run for the front door, and although they'd just come inside, it wouldn't open. He spun, screaming, "Don't hurt me! Don't hurt me! I won't touch her, I swear."

Vince pulled Marsh up from the floor and sat him on the sofa. "I suggest you keep your mouth shut and your threats to yourself," Vince said nervously.

"Am I bleeding?" Marsh cried.

"Not enough to die from," Vince said.

Tara heard the commotion, which served her purpose even better. As soon as she used the bathroom, she began searching through the drawers for something to use as a weapon, but they were empty. The dull ache in her head was a monotonous throb as she walked out.

When she saw the picture on the floor and the fresh blood on the back of Marsh's coat, she gave Millicent a mental high five.

"Did either of you bring the aspirin? My head is hurting."

Dig dug the bottle out of his coat pocket and tossed it to her.

She shook a couple out, set the bottle on a table, and headed toward the open area to the kitchen to look for a glass.

Vince was tired of her and her spook traveling companions and fed up with Marshall Story in so many ways he couldn't count, but he wasn't in a position to challenge Marsh, so he took it out on her.

"You are the brassiest female it has ever been my experience to meet. Technically, you are our prisoner, and yet you are strolling around here like Martha effing Stewart. Make yourself at home, why don't you?"

Tara didn't answer.

Chapter Nine

BEFORE ALLEN COULD get feedback from the OHP, the cop had lost them and was long gone.

After Flynn got the latest clues from Tara about turning off of 51 onto 151 at the Brush Creek sign, they changed their plan and called the Creek County Sheriff and gave them the directions.

"They are dispatching units now, but they cover the entire county with very few patrol cars, so any chance of a timely response is not high," Allen said, as he disconnected.

"Oh my God, please don't let this end bad," Flynn whispered.

Rutherford felt the frustration and fear as much as Flynn. Tara had come through for them so many times. He didn't think he would be able to live with himself if they let her down.

"We haven't lost her. Just keep feeding me info, kid."

Flynn suddenly pointed.

"I see lights in the distance."

Rutherford smiled grimly. "That must be Mannford. We're gaining on them. That's less than thirty minutes behind now. What's the next landmark?"

"The sign to Brush Creek landing, and it will be before we drive into Mannford."

"Keep an eye out, you guys. I'm driving too dang fast on these icy roads here, and I don't have time to sightsee."

Flynn leaned forward from the back seat, and as he did, caught a glimpse of his face in the rearview mirror and nearly didn't recognize himself. He looked older—and dangerous. The glint in his eye and the set of his jaw could be read as "no mercy."

Tara?

He waited, but when she didn't answer, his anxiety increased. What was happening? Why wasn't she answering? Was it already too late?

TARA WAS GOING through cabinets looking for a glass when she heard footsteps. She turned, then dropped the aspirins and faced what she feared was her fate. Marsh and Vince were coming toward her with angry intent.

"What?" she asked.

They stopped a few feet away, but obviously had their fill of the situation and of her. Millicent and Henry had scared them, but not enough to go home without the money.

Marsh pointed at her, shouting in no uncertain terms. "Tune yourself into O' Mara now or whatever the hell it is you do. Tell him if he doesn't tell you where he hid the money, we're getting rid of you and killing his kid just because we can."

Tara's legs went weak so fast she had to grab onto the counter behind her to keep from falling. "No, please! I told you before that I don't have the power to summon spirits. I see them if they are around, and if they're willing, I can talk to them, but there is no threat from this world that will make a spirit do anything."

"You either try, or we've wasted our time here," Marsh said, and started toward her again.

"Stop!" Tara screamed, and backed out from around the kitchen island toward the far end of the room—anything to keep distance between them. "Back off! If I'm going to try this, I need to focus, and threatening me is just negative energy squared! Give me some space."

Marsh wasn't taking any more orders and moved toward her. When he did, it felt as if all the air in the room suddenly shifted, like someone had opened the front door, but when he looked, it was shut.

The hair rose on the back of Tara's arms. She knew what it meant. Spirits were in the house, but she'd never felt it this strongly. When she began to hear Native American drums, she thought she was losing her mind, and over the drum beats she could hear chanting in a language she didn't understand.

Marsh could tell something was happening from the look on her face. "What is it? Do you see O'Mara? Is he telling you where he hid the money?"

She held up her hand for silence, focusing on the voices in her ear. They were chanting louder now, drumming harder and faster until the drum beat matched the heartbeat in her chest.

The air shifted again, and between one breath and the next spirits began to appear, some wearing buckskin and war bonnets trailing down to the floor, others wearing war paint and armed with weapons from long ago. They moved into the space around her, surrounding her until there were so many she couldn't see the faces—only the essence of their beings. Her voice was shaking, her whole body trembling from the impact of the energy around her.

"What's happening?" she whispered. "Who are you?"

We, who have long since passed from the Choctaw Nation, have been summoned to Mynkushi.

Tara was stunned. It sounded like they were saying Minkooshe. Who was that? The Choctaw nation? OMG. Was Nate responsible for this?

"It's cold! Why is it getting so cold in here?" Vince cried.

"Is it O'Mara? Is he here?" Marsh yelled.

Tara blinked, her voice barely above a whisper. "Not O'Mara. Other spirits. Thousands . . . OMG, thousands—"

Marsh was in a panic. He heard her voice shaking, and she was swaying on her feet like she was going to pass out. If she was in a panic, it might be time for him to panic, too. He'd already had one too many run-ins with just her two ghosts, and now she was saying thousands were here. What had they unleashed by wanting her to summon some dead guy up from the grave?

Suddenly, all the glass in the windows exploded outward. The doors flew open and then off their hinges, and the floor on which they were standing began to shake. Everything inside the cabin began to rattle; light fixtures came down from the ceiling, and pictures began falling off the walls.

Marsh dropped to his hands and knees, shouting. "Is it an earthquake?"

Vince was holding on to the end of a kitchen counter, and Dig was on his knees and crawling toward the nearest open door. When they began to hear the drumbeats, Dig bolted to his feet and flew out of the cabin, screaming as he ran toward the pickup.

Tara could see what was happening, but it was as if she were watching a movie, sheltered within the energy around her as surely as if she'd been cradled in her Uncle Pat's arms. The drumbeat was her heartbeat, and her heartbeat was the drumbeat, and she already knew that when the drum stopped, then so would her heart.

Vince had the truck keys in his hand and shouted at Marsh as he bolted for the door. "Run, damn it, run, or I'll leave you behind."

Marsh bolted toward the door, and at the threshold glanced over his shoulder to make sure nothing was following. That was when he saw the girl.

Her eyes were open, but she wasn't moving. Her long dark hair was being blown away from her face, like she was standing in front of a fan, but the air inside the cabin was still. When he realized she was floating a good six inches off the floor, he cleared the porch in two steps, screaming as he ran, "Wait for me! Wait for me!"

Vince was already moving when Marsh caught up and jumped in the pickup. The moment he was in, Vince gunned the engine, spinning snow and mud all over the yard as they headed for the road. They didn't look back.

Tara closed her eyes. She could feel them leaving; going back into the void between their dimension and hers—then a voice in her ear.

Mynkushi! It is done!

The drums stopped. The spirits were gone, taking all the energy with them.

Tara dropped lifelessly to the floor.

THE NEW SUN was finally up and shining straight into Vince's eyes as he drove. He hadn't stopped screaming inside his head, making promises to God that he would change his ways and never do a bad thing again as long as he lived.

Dig was curled up in the back seat with his arms over his head, so scared he could no longer talk, while Marsh couldn't stop.

"She was floating, I tell you! Freaking floating off the floor like some spook in a horror movie! What if they follow us? Oh God, oh God, you didn't see her. I swear she was possessed!"

"Don't cry on my shoulder! You're the one who thought this would be a good idea!" Vince screamed.

"Well, you're the one who agreed to come," Marsh yelled back, and then grabbed at the dash to keep from going through the windshield as Vince suddenly slammed on the brakes.

"What's the matter with you?" Marsh shouted, then saw two Creek County Sheriff cars coming straight at them with lights flashing.

Vince slammed the truck in park and killed the engine.

"What are you doing?" Marsh screamed.

"I'm done! We're done! You just haven't faced it yet."

Vince jumped out of the truck with his hands up as the first car came to a sliding stop, sending a spray of snow into the air. The officers came out with their guns drawn, shouting.

"Get down on your knees! Get down on your knees, and put your hands behind your back!"

"Damn it," Marsh muttered. He got out and dropped.

"Hands behind your back! Do it now!"

The second cop car ejected two more officers who promptly dragged Dig out of the back seat and cuffed him along with his partners, then sat them in the snow at the side of the road. When the deputies realized the girl wasn't with them, they turned to the trio sitting in the snow.

"Where's the girl? Where is Tara Luna?"

RUTHERFORD WAS less than a quarter of a mile behind the last Creek County cop car when they made the turn at the Brush Creek sign and began closing the gap.

"We're almost there," Rutherford said. "Is she talking to you, kid? Can you hear anything?"

Flynn was sick to his stomach. "No. I can't hear anything."

"Talk louder. She's got to be okay," Rutherford said.

Allen was tight-lipped and silent as they sped past the first section line, then the second, and then the third. Up ahead, they could see the patrol cars take a sudden left at two pines, and Flynn took a deep breath.

Where are you, Tara? We're almost there.

He got nothing.

They took the turn onto the private road and kept moving until they came over a small hill and realized both cop cars were stopped, and all three men had been captured and were sitting in the snow in handcuffs.

"Hot damn, they've got them!" Allen said.

Rutherford pulled over and slammed the car into park.

"Where's Tara?" Flynn asked. "I don't see Tara."

Rutherford jumped out. "Where's the girl?" he yelled.

One of the deputies turned around, saw Rutherford coming toward them flashing his badge and then pointed at the men. "She's not here. They keep babbling about ghosts and being haunted and a girl floating off the floor."

Rutherford stomped through the snow to where the perps were sitting.

"Which one of you is Marshall Story?"

Vince and Dig looked at Marsh.

"Thank you for your cooperation," Rutherford said. "Where's the girl?"

Marsh was shaking. "In the house. In the house. Stuff started breaking and blowing up. We ran."

"Son-of-a-bitch!" Rutherford said, and made a run back to the car.

"What's happening?" Flynn asked, as Rutherford jerked the

car in gear.

"Something happened inside the cabin. They left her behind."

The words took the breath from Flynn's body. He couldn't voice what he was thinking for fear it would give power to a truth he couldn't face.

"Can you get around the cars?" Allen asked.

"Just watch me," Rutherford said, and put the SUV in four-wheel drive and headed for the bar ditch. Clearing the parked vehicles in record time, they sped forward, following the narrow road to its end.

As she'd predicted, they saw the old barn first, and seconds later, the A-frame log cabin. They could see the crazy tracks the men left in the snow when they made their getaway. The ruts were over a foot deep where they'd dug out.

Suddenly Flynn was pointing and yelling. "The front door is open! Stop! Stop! Let me out!"

"Hang on, kid," Rutherford said, as he hit the brakes, but Flynn was already out and running toward the cabin before he killed the engine.

Rutherford's hands were shaking. "Oh man, I've never dreaded going inside a crime scene this bad in my life."

Allen wouldn't comment as they ran inside.

Flynn saw her within seconds of entering. She was lying on her side, her arms extended in front of her like she'd been begging for help. There was duct tape wrapped around both wrists and both ankles, although she was no longer bound. He could see dried blood on her clothes and bruises on her face as he dropped to his knees.

"Tara! Tara! Baby, can you hear me?"

He put two fingers on the pulse point at her neck and then rocked back on his heels in shock. There was none.

"Noooo!" he screamed, rolled her over on her back, checked to see if her airway was blocked, then tilted her chin and began performing CPR.

Rutherford dropped down beside her and began doing chest compressions between the exchanges of breath.

Uncertain of the exact address in this rural location, Allen phoned the sheriff to dispatch an ambulance, only to find there was one already on the way.

Flynn went through the motions of CPR just like they'd been taught in physical ed class, concentrating on the act rather than the victim. Yet every time he paused for Rutherford's chest compressions, he would catch a glimpse of the long dark lashes motionless against her skin, the bruise on her cheek, the swollen lip where they'd struck her, and fight the urge to panic.

What felt like an eternity later, Tara gasped, then choked and coughed. He rocked back on his heels.

"Thank you, God."

"She's coming around. Way to go, girl, way to go," Rutherford said, as he felt for a pulse. "We got a pulse! I think we're in luck, kid. I think you just saved her life."

Tears were rolling down Flynn's cheeks, but he didn't know it and wouldn't have cared. He was on his knees beside her, watching the color coming back to her face and those long dark lashes fluttering against her cheeks.

We're here, baby, we're here. Open your eyes.

Flynn.

He cupped her cheek.

I'm here.

"I hear a siren," Allen said, and headed for the door.

Like Flynn, Rutherford was waiting for her to open her eyes.

Then she did—and the moment she saw Flynn she reached toward him, clutching his hand with a death grip. She looked from Flynn to Rutherford, blinking back a sudden rush of tears.

"You found me."

"Are you in pain?" Rutherford asked.

"My head," she said, touching the dark bruise above her brows, then the top of her head.

Rutherford patted her knee. "An ambulance is on the way. Hang in there a couple more minutes."

"Uncle Pat?"

"Oh, right! Hey, Allen. Call Carmichael now, will you? He needs some good news."

"Let me talk," she begged, and tried to sit up.

"Don't move," Allen said, as he made the call. It rang a couple of times before Pat answered.

"Hello?"

"Hey, Pat, it's Detective Allen. I've got someone here who wants to talk to you."

Tara was too shaky to hold the phone so Allen put it on speaker.

"Uncle Pat, they found me. I'm okay."

They all heard the choked sob and then the elation in Pat's voice. "Oh, honey! Thank the Lord. Did they hurt you?"

"I might have a concussion."

"Did they call an ambulance? Are you coming here?"

"Yes, an ambulance is coming."

"Hey, Pat, this is Detective Rutherford. We have you on speaker phone. I'll ask them to transport her to Stillwater, okay?"

"Thank you. Thank all of you for saving my girl."

"It's the kid you have to thank. He can explain when he gets home, but you'll have to hang in there with me on the transport until I can talk to the EMTs. We'll let you know where she winds up."

"Thank you. Tara, honey, I love you, and I'll see you soon, okay?"

"I love you, too."

The moment Pat disconnected, he quickly made a call to Nate Pierce.

"Hello?" Nate said.

Pat could hear drums in the background. The Choctaw had done what Nate said they would do.

"You can tell your people to stop praying. They found her. Other than a concussion, we think she's okay."

The wave of relief that washed through Nate left him weak. "This is good," he said softly.

"And thank you and your people for caring," Pat said.

"I will tell them. Thank you for the call."

Nate dropped the phone in his pocket and went to tell the others. It was going to be a good day.

WHEN THE CALL to Uncle Pat ended, Tara started to get up, but Flynn wouldn't let her.

"Five minutes ago you weren't breathing. Be still."

"I wasn't dead. They just took me with them."

He frowned. "They? And what do you mean, you weren't dead? You didn't have a pulse."

"I mean, I knew I was coming back."

Rutherford got up. "I can't hear this and deal with the world as I know it. I'm going outside to watch for the ambulance."

Allen looked at her in awe and then followed his partner outside.

Flynn's fingers were shaking as he smoothed the hair away from her face. "Did those men—"

"No!" she said abruptly. "They didn't even try. I have Millicent and Henry to thank for giving them plenty else to deal with."

"What happened here?" Flynn said. "The windows . . . all the doors off their hinges . . . what happened here that scared those creeps into running? Was it Millicent and Henry?"

"No. I haven't heard or seen *them* since we got here. OMG. Flynn, you should have seen the others."

"What others?"

"Choctaw spirits. There were hundreds, maybe thousands. They were old, Flynn . . . so old. They said they'd been summoned to protect Mynkushi."

"Who is Mynkushi?"

"It's what they called me, but I don't know what it means. I felt them coming before I heard the drums, then they surrounded me with their energy. Their power was . . . OMG . . . I can't even describe it, but it blew out the windows and doors. They saved me from those men, but you and your crazy-mad skills saved my life."

"Just returning a favor," Flynn said softly and cupped the side of her face.

"Ambulance is here!" Rutherford yelled.

Moments later the cabin was crawling with law enforcement and rescue. Deputies escorted a crime scene team in to gather evidence behind the EMTs who came in for Tara. It didn't take long for them to start an IV, slap an oxygen mask over her mouth, and strap her on a gurney. When they began rolling her out to the waiting ambulance, Flynn ran along beside it.

"Can I go with her?"

"Against the rules, sorry," the EMT said.

"Do you consider her condition critical?" Rutherford asked.

The EMT shook his head. "Her vitals are good, but they'll be checking for a concussion."

"Her uncle has asked for her to be transported to Stillwater Hospital."

"I see no reason to deny," he said.

"Thank you. I'll let him know," Rutherford said.

Flynn got one last glimpse of Tara as the doors closed, and then they were gone.

He headed for the SUV on the run. They wasted no time in leaving. Once again, they were behind her, but this time, they were following her home.

WHEN PAT GOT the news they were on their way back, he called Mona.

"They rescued her. They're on their way to the hospital here in Stillwater."

"Thank the lord! I'll meet you there, okay?"

"Yes, and Mona . . ."

"What, honey?"

"Thank you for being here for me. I wouldn't have made it without you."

"It's what you do for the people you love."

Pat took a deep breath and closed his eyes, letting the words wrap around his heart. "For the people you love?"

"Yes, like you and Tara, and don't get all in a panic. I didn't commit you to anything except maybe a hug."

He grinned. "I can handle that. See you soon," he said and ran to get showered and changed.

Chapter Ten

THE AMBULANCE RIDE back to Stillwater was the end of a nightmare. The EMT kept talking to her, judging her ability to comprehend and answer against the side-effects of a possible concussion or a more serious head injury.

Between answering his questions, trying not to stare at Henry who was floating up near the ceiling, and talking to Millicent, she wasn't getting any rest.

"Are you doing okay, Tara? Are you still cold?" the EMT asked.

"A little," she said. He promptly got another blanket and added it to the one already on her. "Thank you. That feels good."

He gave her shoulder a quick pat, unaware Henry was floating right above him blowing kisses at Tara. She had to close her eyes to keep from laughing. Then she heard Millicent's voice, and she heard something she'd never heard from her before. Fear.

You need to take some self-defense classes. This can't ever happen again.

Tara shuddered. *Trust me. I don't want a repeat, but knowing karate won't protect me from a Taser.*

Silence.

Millicent?

I do not approve of this century's weapons of choice.

But this is the century I live in, so I'm stuck with what's here, right?

Tara heard a snort.

Logic is highly over-rated.

Tara stifled a grin. Millicent did not like to be thwarted.

You're different now. You know that, don't you?

Tara frowned. *Different how?*

Those spirits who saved you were very old and very powerful. Henry and I couldn't even get close to you. It was terribly frightening for us.

But why am I different?

It's what you came back with . . . what they gave you. Besides the abilities you were born with, you now have the ability to see into people's hearts. You will know when people lie. You will see their evil, and you will see the good. It is something rare and very valuable, my child, and it is your responsibility to use it in the service of others.

Tara frowned. My child? Millicent had never called her that before. Why did—understanding dawned. "OMG."

The EMT looked down. "Are you okay? Are you in pain?"

"No."

Millicent!

Silence.

Henry!

Nowhere to be seen.

Flynn heard her. *Tara? What's wrong?*

OMG. Flynn! Millicent was talking to me and referred to me as her child.

Well, she helped raise you, right?

She NEVER said that before. EVER.

So what's the big—Oh. Wow! Really? Your Mother? Does this mean Henry might be your father, too?

I don't know, but I will find out.

Don't be mad that you didn't know before. Think about it. You can't tell a little kid stuff like that.

Silence.

Tara?

I'm here. I'm thinking.

Think about me while you're at it, because I'm sure thinking about you.

Tara closed her eyes. Flynn O'Mara was fast becoming the second most important person in her life. It was something to sleep on, and she did.

"THERE THEY COME!" Pat said, pointing to an ambulance pulling up to the ER entrance. Even though Pat now knew Tara was safe, he didn't relax until he saw her face.

Mona was clutching his hand, anxious to see *both* of their children.

Tara squinted against the bright light of day as they wheeled her out of the ambulance, but when she saw her uncle waiting, she struggled not to cry. For a time, she'd been certain she would never see him again, and she reached desperately for his hand as they wheeled her past.

"Uncle Pat!"

"Tara . . . sweetheart. Thank God, thank God!" he said, as he ran along beside her.

"Welcome back, honey," Mona said, then saw the bruises and swelling on Tara's face and bit her lip to keep from crying as Pat followed them inside.

The detectives pulled up a couple of minutes behind the ambulance. Flynn jumped out on the run and went straight to his mom and hugged her.

She threw her arms around him fiercely. "Don't ever scare me like this again, okay?"

Rutherford caught the look she gave them and could see she was upset that they'd taken Flynn along. He glanced at the kid. "She doesn't know, does she?"

Flynn shook his head.

Mona frowned. "Know what?"

Rutherford shrugged. "That's his story to tell."

Flynn sighed. "Come with me, Mom. We need to talk."

He led her off into the waiting area as the ER team began assessing Tara's condition. Pat had given them her medical history earlier, and thanks to a heads up from the EMT team transporting her, they had a portable x-ray waiting.

Once again, everything happening to Tara was out of her control. She followed their orders, answered their questions, reassuring everyone again that she had not been molested, and wanted all of this to be over, and for her life to be back to normal—at least her version of normal.

But then she remembered Millicent's warning. She'd come back different. Like she wasn't already different enough? Now she was also a walking, talking, lie-detector/exorcist? She didn't want to be seeing the evil in people. She wasn't even eighteen years old yet. OMG! What was up with that?

"Okay, Tara. You said the kidnappers Tased you on the leg," Doctor Cash asked.

"Yes. I turned around to run and then felt pain on the back of my left leg and went down. That's *the* most painful thing ever. I couldn't think or move." The re-telling was enough to leave her voice shaky and thick with tears.

"We better take a look at that," Cash said, and then saw the detectives in the hall trying to get his attention and excused himself. "Nurse, remove her jeans, and I'll be right back."

When the nurse came at Tara with a pair of surgical shears, she groaned. The jeans were old, but she didn't have that many pairs.

"Do you have to cut them?" Tara asked. "I can take them off."

The nurse smiled. "Oh, we won't ruin your jeans, honey. All we're gonna do is turn this pair into summer shorts. Now, how far up on your leg did they Taser you?" the nurse asked, as they rolled her over onto her side.

Tara pointed to about halfway between her hip and knee and then listened to the snip of the scissors as they cut through the fabric to reveal the small wounds.

When Doctor Cash came back, he eyed Tara curiously and then inspected the small burn wounds, which didn't seem to be infected.

"When can I go home?" Tara asked.

"Not tonight, for sure. I was just informed that when the detectives found you, you weren't breathing."

Shock swept through Pat so fast he staggered. "Oh my God! Tara! Is that true?"

"I don't know. I don't remember anything except leaving with the spirits."

Doctor Cash frowned. "Excuse me?"

Tara sighed. "After we got to the cabin, the men got angry

because I kept telling them I couldn't find what they were looking for. When they came at me, I became surrounded by a couple of centuries' worth of Choctaw spirits. They kept the kidnappers away from me, and in the meantime scared them enough that they all ran away, leaving me behind."

The doctor was listening, but she could tell he thought she'd been hallucinating as a result of her head injury.

"So, if the kidnappers ran off, then how did you wind up on the floor of that cabin without a pulse?"

Tara felt like screaming. "This is so frustrating and complicated, trying to make people understand my life. Look, all I know is that when the spirits left, they took me with them. Maybe my body wasn't breathing because I was so far away, but I wasn't dead. I knew all the time I was coming back."

Cash's eyes narrowed, then he turned and pointed to one of the nurses.

"Get Doctor Vernon on the phone."

"Who's Doctor Vernon?" Pat asked.

"He's the head of Psychiatry here at—"

Tara hit the bed with her fists, rattling the IV on the pole and making the other machines they'd hooked her up to beep and alarm.

"No! Look, Doctor Cash, the bottom line is that I'm a freak. I see and talk to ghosts, and no shrink is going to change that."

The doctor's eyes widened. "Wait! Are you *that* Tara . . . from the tornado?"

"Yes."

His lips parted, and he took a deep breath.

"Cancel the call to Vernon." He stared at Tara curiously. "Choctaw spirits? Seriously?"

She nodded.

"Freakin' amazing," he muttered. "But you're still staying overnight."

Tara sighed. "Okay."

AFTER SETTLING Tara into her room, cleaning her up, and feeding her for the first time since she'd been taken, she'd quickly fallen asleep from exhaustion. Pat went to dinner with Mona and Flynn and got one more bit of news along with his food.

Mona glanced at Flynn. "Tell him what you told me."

Flynn sighed. His mother had freaked. He had no idea how Pat would react, but it had to be told.

"What's wrong?" Pat asked.

"Nothing is wrong. But I haven't told Mom or you what happened to me after I woke up from the coma."

Pat frowned. "Are you okay, Flynn? If you have problems, we can get help."

Flynn stared at him just a moment and then spoke. "No, I'm not blacking out. I'm not having seizures, and I have no memory loss."

Pat's eyes widened.

"And no, this isn't a trick. What happened to me, changed me."

Pat looked at Mona in disbelief.

"Yes, he's reading our thoughts. In fact, he can hear everyone's thoughts, and it's driving him crazy. Tara has been helping him learn how to focus and block. And here I thought all I had to worry about was his GPA."

Flynn shrugged. "It's not my fault."

Pat shook his head in amazement, and then in a gesture of understanding, put his hand on Flynn's shoulder. "You don't know it yet, but you have just been given the answer to every man's prayer."

Flynn frowned. "Like what? This isn't a joke."

"No joke, son. Think about it. It's been the downfall of man ever since woman entered the picture. We never know what we do wrong and never know what they are thinking. But you do. Wow. If you play your cards right, you'll never make a wrong move as long as you live."

Flynn grinned. "I never thought of it that way."

Mona rolled her eyes as the waiter arrived at their table.

"Is everybody ready to order now?"

Pat grinned and then pointed at Flynn.

"He's ordering for all of us."

Flynn laughed, and just like that, the thing he'd feared most had come off without a hitch.

MILLICENT WAS standing at the end of Tara's bed, staring at the girl who was turning a woman. Henry was beside her. The secret they'd kept from Tara for all these years was out. The question now was what to do about it?

Henry, what are we going to do?

He shrugged.

You're no help.

He spun into the corner of the room with his arms folded and frowned.

We knew this day would come, right? And we owe it to her to be truthful, right?

Henry nodded.

Fine. Then it's settled. We answer whatever questions she asks. She's waking up and—Drat! Company's coming. Later.

Tara opened her eyes and rolled over onto her back just as someone knocked on her door. "Come in," she called out.

The door opened, and Nate Pierce entered. He went straight toward her without speaking, stopping at the foot of her bed.

"You should have let me take you home."

She sighed. "You are so right."

"You are okay?"

"Yes, but I need to talk to you about what happened."

"I'm listening."

"Your ancestors saved me," Tara said.

Even though they'd prayed for this to happen, the fact that it had and she knew it was surprising. He managed to pull himself together and moved closer. "The tribe beat the drums, asking the Old Ones to watch over you."

Tara grabbed his hand and started to cry. "They came in a burst of light, with so much energy it blew the doors open and all of the glass out of the windows where I was being held. There were thousands and thousands . . . so many I couldn't see faces, only shapes and they said they had been summoned to protect Mynkushi. Who is that? What does it have to do with coming to me?"

Nate's voice was shaking. "They came for you. They have given you a name . . . Little Moon."

"Oh, wow," she whispered, and leaned back against the pillows as the tears rolled down her face.

"Are you okay? Do you want me to go?" Nate asked.

"No. You're the only one who can help me make sense of the rest of it."

He looked startled. "There's more?"

"When they left, they took me with them. I had no pulse when Flynn and the detectives found me."

His hands were shaking. "I need to sit down," he said, and pulled up a chair.

Tara's voice grew soft with awe and wonder. "There are other dimensions in time and space. I saw and understood everything they wanted me to see. There are no words in this world to describe what I saw, and there are no colors here that compare to what was there. They kept telling me that I had a task in this world that would not be easy, but that I would succeed because my heart was pure."

Nate shook his head in disbelief. "I hear you talking and feel like I should be on my knees in prayer. You are a blessing to all who know you, Tara Luna, and I am proud to call you my friend."

"Thank you for sending them, because they kept me safe until my rescuers arrived."

He bowed his head. "You are most welcome, but there is something you need to understand. When the Old Ones named you, they gave you a Choctaw soul to live in harmony with the one already within you. You will be welcome in both the world of the white man and the world of the First People. I will still call you Tara, but our people will know you as Mynkushi. You are a sister to me. It is so."

Tara smiled. "Before I only had Uncle Pat, and now I have the whole Choctaw tribe as family?"

"Pretty much," he said, and briefly touched the top of her head. "You should rest. You know where I am if you need me. Welcome back, Mynkushi."

And just like that, he was gone, leaving Tara speechless and struggling to understand the ramifications of what he'd told her. It made what Millicent said about the gift she'd come back with a little easier to understand, but she still didn't know what she was supposed to do with it.

She closed her eyes and then felt Millicent on the bed beside her. There were so many questions rolling around in her head, but the only one that mattered was the one that came out of her mouth.

"Are you and Henry the spirits of my parents?"

Yes.

"OMG."

Are you mad?

"Well, no," Tara said, and then burst into tears.

THE WHOLE REST of the day, Tara felt them near her. Even when she couldn't see or hear them, she knew they were there. Doctors came and went while Uncle Pat sat by her bed.

Every now and then she'd catch him looking at her with tears in his eyes. She knew he felt guilty because all this had happened, but the bottom line was, there was nothing he could have done to protect her. It was a sad state of affairs that psychics could use their powers to help everyone else but themselves.

Mona and Flynn had come and gone twice. Once to bring Pat something he needed from home, and once bringing Tara a chocolate malt from Braum's Ice Cream store. With a mouth too sore and swollen to chew, she'd downed it a spoonful at a time while Flynn watched her without speaking.

He heard her thoughts. He knew about Millicent and Henry, and that she was both elated to know they had never left her, but devastated she would never be able to hug them or see them as they'd been. They'd taken on personalities from their past on purpose so as not to give themselves away until she was old enough to process it. He also knew that she had already decided never to tell Pat. He'd earned the parent status by sticking with her all these years, and she didn't ever want him to feel less than that.

When he and his mother finally left, she'd looked at him once, acknowledging that she'd "let" him into her sadness and trusted him to keep the secrets.

Rutherford and Allen showed up late in the afternoon to check on her and give her an update. Rutherford was carrying a stuffed white teddy bear, and Allen had a box of chocolates.

When she saw them come in with the presents, she smiled.

"My heroes," she said.

They both grinned.

Rutherford handed her the bear. "We named him Spooky, seeing as how you're always surrounded by them."

"Hospital food usually sucks," Allen said, and handed her the chocolates.

"Thank both of you so much. Thank you for always believing my crazy phone calls, and thank you for coming to my rescue."

They seemed embarrassed as Pat added his thanks.

"There are no words to express my gratitude," Pat said.

"You'll be happy to know that the three kidnappers have pled guilty and are safely in jail. They'll do their time in the States and be old men if and when they ever get out."

"Thank God," Pat said.

At that moment, both detectives' cell phones went off.

"Duty calls," they said. "Get well soon."

"Thank you again, and thank you for my presents," Tara said, as the door closed behind them. She handed the candy to her uncle. "Open this for me, and we'll both eat a piece."

He began peeling the cellophane wrapping off the box.

"You know that the only thing you've eaten today was a chocolate malt, and now you're going for chocolate candy."

"Sounds like the perfect menu to me," she said, and then stifled a giggle when Henry popped up at the foot of her bed and looked longingly at the box. Henry did love candy.

When she felt the rush of Millicent's presence around her shoulders, she knew she was getting a hug.

Love you guys.

We love you, too.

She heard a pop, saw a faint puff of pink smoke, and sighed. Life was almost back to normal.

She'd missed the first day of the last semester of her senior year, and by the end of the day, everyone at Stillwater High School knew why.

After that, flowers and balloons began arriving at the hospital, and then her BFFs Nikki, Mac, and Penny came by, filling her in on all the latest while Uncle Pat made himself absent so they could talk freely.

She leaned back in the bed with a smile on her face, listening absently to their chatter with a sense of awe. So this was what it felt like to really belong in a place. It was a good thing.

WHEN SHE WENT home the next day, Mona and Flynn were waiting for her at the house, and every evening throughout the rest of the week, Mona and Flynn came over, helping out with chores that had been hers. It was beginning to feel like a routine, and it was turning them into a family. Even with the thing between her and Flynn, it felt right.

Tara could see how much Mona meant to her uncle and guessed that, if nothing happened to change the situation, after she and Flynn graduated and started college, married or not, Pat and Mona would be living under one roof.

It was the following Saturday before the DEA showed up at their place looking for Mona. One agent was very familiar. It was the undercover agent with the crazy scar on his face who'd saved Tara and Flynn from drowning after their wreck.

FLYNN WAS CARRYING in groceries while Pat and Mona were putting them up. Tara was stretched out on the sofa, snug and warm under her OSU afghan and still relegated to patient status. She was watching Flynn as he came and went, checking out the way his arms and shoulders were filling out and thinking what a big guy her guy was turning out to be. He'd just gone back into the kitchen when she saw a dark SUV pull up in the driveway.

"Someone's here!" she yelled.

Pat came back to answer the knock and opened it to a duo of DEA agents flashing their badges.

"We need to speak to Mona O'Mara. She said to meet her here."

"Yes. Come in," Pat said. "Have a seat. I'll go get her."

They both eyed Tara, but one more curious than the other.

Tara recognized him on sight. "Hey. I know you," she said.

French Langdon grinned, which made the scar on his cheek pull slightly at one corner of his mouth. "Looks like you're still getting in trouble," he said. "We heard what happened. How are you doing?"

"I'm fine. Did you go on that fishing trip?"

He shook his head. "No farther than my father's farm pond. I know a good tip when I hear it."

Flynn walked into the room, took one look at the agents, and frowned. Tara saw the look and sent him a message.

What's the matter with you?

He thinks you're hot.

He saved your life, remember?

That doesn't mean I ignore the fact he lusts for you.

So. He really thinks I'm hot?

It was the sexy drawl in her voice that shocked Flynn. He turned to face her, saw the glitter in her eyes, and realized she was teasing him.

He glared. *You are so going to pay for that.*

Tara arched an eyebrow. *Promises, promises.*

"I've got one more sack of groceries to bring in," he muttered, and gave her a look as he walked past.

She grinned. That would teach him to head hop on thoughts, then she saw Mona walk in. Tara could tell she was nervous.

The agents stood up, suddenly all business.

"Mrs. O'Mara?"

"Yes."

"Might we have a few words with you?"

"Come with me," she said, and took them back into the kitchen.

The moment Flynn came back and found them gone, he leaned over the sofa and kissed her.

"Thank you, but what was that for?" she asked.

"A reminder that I was the first one who noticed you were hot. I don't want you to forget."

Before she could answer, something happened. Something she'd never felt before—an overwhelming shift of consciousness. For a few moments, she weighed nothing, saw nothing but a bright white light, and felt nothing but an overwhelming sense of being safe and loved.

That's it, Tara. That's the gift.

Millicent?

Yes. You just felt Flynn's intent. That's when you know this is someone you can trust.

OMG.

Flynn frowned. "Who are you talking to?" he asked.

"Millicent."

"Oh." He shrugged. "Tell her I said hello."

"You tell her yourself. I'm going to the kitchen. I want to find out where that dang money is that nearly got the both of us killed."

They walked in just as Mona was getting into the details.

"I can't tell you exactly, but I know what it means. He said it's with Aunt Tillie," Mona said.

"So, where does his Aunt Tillie live?" Langdon asked.

"Technically, she's no kin to him at all. She was just a nice old woman who lived in the house behind us when we were newlyweds. And if he left it with her, then that means it's in the Fairlawn Cemetery here in Stillwater, because Tillie Walters is long since dead. Her plot is in the oldest part of the cemetery. She was buried next to her husband, but I don't remember his name."

"Man! After all this drama, the answer is almost too easy. This is great!" Langdon said. "I think we have all we need. We'll let you know if it's there."

"It will be there," Tara said. "The dead don't lie."

French eyed her curiously, wondering what it would be like to be her, then saw the look on Flynn's face and got the message loud and clear. She was definitely hands off.

"If there's nothing else, I'll see you to the door," Flynn said.

Tara grinned. Flynn was ready to get rid of them.

The agents stood up.

"Thank you for your help. We'll be in touch," Langdon said.

Flynn followed them to the door, opened it, and politely stepped back. "Happy digging," he said.

Langdon grinned. "You got yourself a handful, kid, but you are one lucky dude."

"I know that," Flynn said, then waited until they were both clear of the threshold before he added, "No, I couldn't take you in a fair fight . . . yet."

Langdon spun. The stunned look on his face only added to the moment. "How did you—"

"You don't want to know," Flynn said, and closed the door in their faces.

He was grinning when he turned around, then realized Tara was standing there with her hands on her hips.

"Uh—"

"I was not spying on you. Your mom and Uncle Pat are in the kitchen kissing. I have nowhere else to be."

He rolled his eyes. "Thanks for the visual."

"So, what are you waiting for?" she asked.

He opened his arms as she stepped into the embrace.

As always, for Tara, it felt like a homecoming.

"You make me crazy," Flynn said.

"Then kiss me before you lose what's left of your mind," Tara whispered.

So he did.

IT WAS THE next day before they got the news, and it put an end to all their worries.

Mona had just taken the last piece of fried chicken from the skillet. Tara was setting the table, and Flynn was putting ice in the glasses.

"Supper is ready," Mona said.

Tara smiled. "This is a treat. Usually I'm the one cooking. Uncle Pat will think he's in heaven."

Pat walked in on that comment. "I'm already in heaven. I have the people I care most about within my sight, and something smells good."

Before Mona could comment, her cell phone, which was on the counter near where Flynn was working, began to ring.

Flynn glanced down. "Hey, Mom. You might want to take this. It's the DEA."

Mona glanced at Pat and then wiped her hands and picked up the phone. "Hello."

"Mrs. O'Mara, this is Agent Langdon. I would like to speak to you one more time. Are you available?"

"I guess, but I'm not at home. I'm at Tara's house."

"Do you mind if I stop by? It won't take but a few minutes."

"Do you mean now? We're just about to sit down to supper."

"I'm just a block from the house. I promise this won't take more than a couple of minutes. I have something to tell you and something to give you."

"Yes, I guess," she said, and disconnected.

"Sorry, everyone, but that was Agent Langdon. He said he had something to tell me and something to give me, and he's a couple of minutes away."

"Hey. No problem," Pat said. "If it has to do with putting all of this money stuff behind us, then so much the better."

Tara put the chicken back to stay warm and put the lids back on the vegetables she'd been ready to take up, and while she was working, there was a knock at the door.

"He's already here," Mona said. "All of you. Come with me. Whatever it is, it's news for us all."

Pat opened the door. "Come in."

"I apologize for the abrupt visit, but I'm on my way out of town and wanted to let you know that we found the money."

"Thank goodness," Mona said. "Now this can be over."

"There's just one other thing," Langdon said, and took an envelope out of his pocket and handed it to Mona. "This was on top of the money. It's addressed to you. Of course we did not open it because whatever it says, has nothing to do with us. I'm sorry we met under such dire circumstances, but it has truly been a pleasure meeting you all." He glanced at Flynn and smiled. "Even if our first meeting was rather wet."

Flynn nodded. "And for that I am forever grateful."

"Have a nice evening . . . and for that matter, have a nice rest of your lives."

Mona sat down and tore into the envelope as Langdon drove away.

"I can't imagine what—"

A key fell out of the envelope onto the hardwood floor. Flynn bent down and picked it up. "This is a weird-looking key."

"It looks like a safety deposit box key," Mona said, and opened the letter that was inside.

She scanned it briefly, then gasped. "Dear Lord!" she cried, and started to cry.

Pat sat down beside her. "What's wrong, honey? If it's something bad we will—"

"It's not bad. It's good. It's better than good. Just listen," she said, as she read aloud.

Dear Mona,

If you're reading this, then you know the worst. I never intended for things to get so messed up. You and Flynn were my world until the drugs. All I can say is how sorry I am for screwing everything up. The key goes to a safety deposit box at the bank downtown. It's the one we used together. Your name is still on the account, so you won't have any trouble getting access. There's a little over $40,000 in the box that I saved for Flynn's college. It's not drug money. I swear to God. I won it at the Cherokee Casino about two months after you moved out. I can't do anything else for Flynn, but I can pay for his education. Tell him I'm sorry and that he's the best thing we ever did together.

Michael.

Flynn was in shock, and at the same time, feeling guilty. The last thing he'd said to his dad had been in anger.

Tara slipped her hand in his and gave it a squeeze. "He knows you didn't mean it," she said softly.

"But that's just it, Tara. At the time, I meant every bit of it. He destroyed our family."

"But at his worst, he was still thinking of you," Pat said. "You gotta give him that. Trust me, I know about letting people down. I've done it to Tara over and over for years, and she kept forgiving me and trusting me to get better. I just happened to live along enough for that to happen. Your dad didn't get that break. Understand?"

Flynn's shoulders slumped. "Yeah, I do."

"This is quite a gift," Pat added.

Flynn looked up at his mom. She was in tears, but they were

happy tears.

"This is a gift from God, Flynn. I didn't know how we were going to pay for college, and now it's a done deal. Regardless of every other bad thing he did, I bless him for this."

"*If* the money is still in the box," Flynn said.

Tell him it's there.

Tara jumped. "Millicent says it's there."

"Oh, wow." He started smiling. "This is amazing."

"And supper is getting cold!" Tara said. "Let's go heat the stuff up and celebrate this good news with some of your mom's fried chicken."

Chapter Eleven

TARA WAS STILL awake long after she'd gone to bed, thinking about all that had happened in the short time they'd been here. All the things she had experienced in her seventeen years had been preparing her for this time and for what was to come. For a couple of Gypsies who had always been on the move, she and Pat had put down very strong roots in a very short time.

But it was the realization that she'd never *really* lost her parents that was the most overwhelming. She kept remembering Connie who died from carbon monoxide poisoning, seeing the little spirit's panic when she feared her family would not be saved, feeling the love she had for them. It was proof to Tara that love survived everything—even death and separation.

Tara heard a pop and then felt the air in the room shift as her two ghosts entered this dimension.

You can't sleep. Are you sick? Do you hurt? Should I wake Pat up?

"I'm fine, and OMG, *no*, don't wake up Uncle Pat unless you want to give him a heart attack. I was just thinking."

There was a long moment of silence, and then Henry popped up at the foot of her bed wearing a long nightgown and an old-fashioned sleeping cap. It was a far cry from the coonskin cap and the suit of armor.

She pointed. "What's with Henry and the old-fashioned nightgown?"

He thinks it will help make you sleepy.

Tara smiled. "I so love you guys."

Henry put his hands over his heart and then pointed at her, while Millicent did her little swirl around Tara's shoulders, which was as close to a ghostly hug as she could get.

Have you thought about what you're going to do with your gift?

Tara leaned back against the pillows. "It's all I have thought about these days. I don't want to waste it."

You won't. When it comes to you, you will know that it's right. You should sleep now.

Tara glanced at the clock. It was almost one a.m.

"Yes, you're right about that. Good night, you guys, and thanks for stopping by."

Tara rolled over on her side, pulled the covers up close around her ears, and closed her eyes. She felt the slight give on the mattress that told her Millicent wasn't leaving until she slept. It felt good to be loved.

A BIG YELLOW moon cast an eerie glow on a house at the far edge of town. *The house was on its last legs. No screens or curtains on the windows, and there was a hole in the front porch just to the left of the front door. It wasn't a place Tara had ever seen before and didn't know why she was there. Inside, she heard the sound of violence, then a woman screaming obscenities and children crying.*

She knocked on the door, but no one answered. When she looked in the window, she saw a man and woman fighting and three little children huddled together in a corner of the room. The oldest one, a child of no more than ten, was sheltering his younger siblings within his bruised and too-skinny arms. While the younger children's faces were swollen from crying and their cheeks streaked with tears, his expression was blank. The light in his eyes was long dimmed from witnessing too many nights such as this.

Tara felt the woman's hopelessness as she fought to protect herself and her children, but it was the man who impacted her most of all.

She'd already experienced part of her new gift, learning how to recognize the good in people, but this was the first time she was experiencing the physical impact of being in the presence of evil.

The night's darkness seeped into her soul, turning off every emotion except fear. She could hear whispers and cackles of evil laughter and screams from another realm of existence she never wanted to see. She couldn't move. She couldn't breathe. It wasn't until the man turned away that the spell was broken, and when it lifted, she turned to run, then remembered the children and looked back. They couldn't run. They had nowhere to go.

All of a sudden she heard Millicent's voice.

Now you know.

SHE WOKE UP with a gasp, her heart pounding, her hands shaking as she thrust them through the tangles in her hair.

"OMG!"

Tara! Are you okay?

Flynn! Yes. It was just a bad dream.

I could feel your fear. What happened? Did you have another premonition?

No. It was a horrible nightmare, but it had a message I've been waiting for.

Tell me.

I know what I'm going to do with my life.

You mean, besides spend the rest of it with me?

Tara's heart skipped a beat. *What are you saying?*

Later. For now, just tell me what you want to do when you graduate from college.

I am going to work for the welfare department. I want to be an advocate for children who can't speak for themselves. I will know when their environment is wrong . . . when they live with evil. They won't even have to tell me what's happening. I'll know. I can save them, Flynn. I can make a difference.

Silence, then his voice. *That's perfect. You find the bad people, and I'll arrest them. We'll be the deadliest duo since Batman and Robin ever!*

Tara smiled. *Okay, I told you. Now you tell me what you meant by me and the rest of your life.*

I guess I'm asking you if you love me as much as I love you.

Tara pulled her knees up beneath her chin and shivered with sudden longing.

If you can truly read my mind, then you already know the answer.

There was a long moment of silence, then his voice again—in her heart.

Together forever, Moon Girl?

Together forever, Flynn O'Mara. We'll be lunatics together. Imagine. Two times the lunatics and in one place.

Unbeatable. I like that, Moon Girl.

Tara kissed her hand, then raised it to her lips and blew.

Did you feel that?

Feel what?

I just blew you a kiss. She heard him chuckle.

Ah. I wondered what that was, but you know there's way more to this thing between us than kisses.

This time it was Tara with the long moment of silence, and then she answered.

If it's with you, it will always be right. I trust you implicitly. Go to sleep, Flynn O'Mara, and dream of me.

Always in my heart. Always in my mind.

Her heart was pounding as she slid down beneath the covers and closed her eyes. The heat kicked on inside the house, moving the feathers on the dream catcher over her bed.

Monday she would be back in school, and come graduation she and Flynn would step into a new part of life.

Stronger together, and no longer alone in this lunatic life she called her own.

The End

About Sharon Sala

Sharon Sala's stories are often dark, dealing with the realities of this world, and yet she's able to weave hope and love within the words for the readers who clamor for her latest works.

Her books repeatedly make the big lists, including The New York *Times*, *USA Today*, and *Publisher's Weekly*, and she's been nominated for a RITA seven times, which is the romance writer's equivalent of having an OSCAR or an EMMY nomination. Always an optimist in the face of bad times, many of the stories she writes come to her in dreams, but there's nothing fanciful about her work. She puts her faith in God, still trusts in love and the belief that, no matter what, everything comes full circle.

Visit her at sharonsalabooks.com and on Facebook.

CPSIA information can be obtained at www.ICGtesting.com
Printed in the USA
BVOW02s0540161013

333884BV00001B/131/P